To Honour the Dead

To Honour the Dead

John Dean

ROBERT HALE · LONDON

© John Dean 2012
First published in Great Britain 2012

ISBN 978-0-7198-0701-5

Robert Hale Limited
Clerkenwell House
Clerkenwell Green
London EC1R 0HT

www.halebooks.com

2 4 6 8 10 9 7 5 3 1

Typeset in 11/14.5pt New Century Schoolbook
Printed in Great Britain by the MPG Books Group,
Bodmin and King's Lynn

Of course, thought Jack Harris, as he sat with his feet up on the desk in his dimly lit office, it could be that he really was the only one who sensed that something was wrong. Perhaps, thought the detective chief inspector, the others simply could not feel it or, even if they could, did not share his concerns. What if, and the thought came to Harris reluctantly, as it always did with suggestions of personal weakness, he *was* overreacting? Harris knew that most of his colleagues at Levton Bridge Police Station shared that view; he had seen it in their faces every time he started to talk about it. For all their scepticism, the nagging sensation would not go away. It was not a fleeting thought, either. Harris had felt like this for weeks, months even, the unease at its strongest in his quietest moments. Tonight, in the silence of his office, it was more powerful than ever and, with a sigh, he lowered his feet to the floor and walked over to stare moodily out of the window.

Looking onto the deserted street, the inspector had to acknowledge that it was difficult to rationalize his concerns about rising tension in the valley; it was not as if he could see people locked in furious combat down on the pavement. And it *had* just been one woman shouting her mouth off, after all. A crazy woman who had been incapable, in the inspector's view, of rational thought for months, consumed by the belief that her teenage son had been murdered.

Like his colleagues, Harris was convinced that the boy's death was an accident and that his team had done everything by the book. That was not what worried the inspector; what concerned him was Esther Morritt's constant barrage of criticism and innuendo. Harris knew that it did not take much to stir ferment in the small, tight-knit communities ranged along the North Pennines valley. On the other hand, no one else believed that she had created an atmosphere of ferment.

'Maybe I'm the one who's going crazy,' he said, glancing down at the two dogs lying by the warmth of the radiator. They watched him with interest. 'No, that's not it.'

Besides, he thought, as he made his way out of the first-floor office, dogs at his heels, there *had* been signs that tensions were increasing in the days leading up to tomorrow's inquest. For starters, thought the inspector as he walked down the stairs, trying to avoid the dogs as they barged past him in the gloom, his sergeant, Matty Gallagher, who had led the investigation, had been more irritable than usual. Harris turned right at the bottom of the stairs and entered the control room.

'All quiet?' he asked, glancing at the two operators.

'As the grave,' said one of the women, nodding. She noticed his sceptical expression. 'You expecting something, sir? No one told us you had an op on.'

'We haven't,' said Harris, turning and walking out of the door. 'Good night, ladies.'

When Harris had gone, the operator turned to her colleague.

'He's not getting any better,' she said.

'Rang up from home three times last night shift I did. I have no idea what he thinks is going to happen.'

'Matty Gallagher reckons he's expecting a riot or something.'

'Does Matty agree?'

'Course not – says it's all in the DCI's head.'

'It's living alone on that hillside, that does it,' said the operator slyly. 'Him and his whisky bottle.'

Her voice seemed a touch loud and, instinctively, both operators glanced at the door but the inspector had already gone. Having walked past the front counter and murmured a farewell to the officer on duty, he headed out into the early evening chill, the frost already beginning to glisten on the pavements. Within a couple of minutes, the inspector was driving past the park when movement caught his eye. He brought the vehicle to a halt, cut the engine and wound the window down. He sat for a few moments, resting his elbows on the steering wheel and staring into the darkness, seeking further movement in among the trees. Voices carried on the night air towards him, teenagers' voices, and as he watched, a group of five or six young people emerged from a side street, a couple carrying white carrier bags. Hearing the clink of bottles and seeing the teenagers disappear into the park, the inspector reached for his radio.

'Control,' said the female operator's voice.

'It's Harris. Just seen some teenagers heading into the park.'

There was a pause.

'You still there, Myra?' asked the inspector.

'Yes, sorry, sir. Lost you for a second there. I'll get uniform to have a look.'

'Thank you,' said Harris, starting the engine. 'You can never be too careful.'

'No, sir. Good night, sir.'

'Good night, Myra.'

When the sound of the inspector's vehicle had receded into the distance, a figure emerged from behind one of the trees in the park. He was holding a petrol can. After glancing nervously around, he set off along the perimeter path, pausing to stare over the low stone wall into the churchyard, its headstones faintly illuminated by the glow from the nearby street lights. The man gave a slight shudder and continued along the path until he reached the British Legion's wooden bowls pavilion. After pausing for a few moments to listen to the town clock striking seven, the man unscrewed the lid from the can and started to pour petrol at the base of one of the walls. Satisfied that enough had been applied, he reached into a coat pocket to produce a box of matches. Striking one of them, he watched in fascination as the flame flared. He was about to drop the match onto the petrol when he heard voices over by one of the flower beds on the far side of the park. Peering into the darkness, he could just about make out a small group of teenagers, drinking from cans of lager. He saw the glow of a cigarette.

'Shit,' he murmured.

The flame flickered and died out and the man cursed beneath his breath as he dropped the match. He fumbled in his pocket for another one but a change in the teenagers' voices alerted him and he saw two torch beams by the entrance to the park. As two uniformed police officers approached, the teenagers scattered, laughing and shouting, and the man made his way back unseen along the shadows of the perimeter path. At the churchyard wall, he hesitated before climbing over to crouch among the headstones. He could hear the officers' voices carried on the still night air as they approached the pavilion.

'Looks like another of the DCI's wild-goose chases,' said Roger Barnett, a grey-haired officer in his early fifties. 'That man has not got enough to do, if you ask me. God knows why he's interested in the park. Come on, we've checked it, let's get out of here.'

'Shouldn't we at least have a look round, Sarge?' asked his young female companion. 'I mean, just to be sure?'

'Why bother? They'll have all legged it by now.'

'We might find a clue as to who they were.'

'Who cares?' said Barnett. 'Listen, love, when I was working down in Roxham, we were too busy to bother with kids mucking about. Proper policing that was. Not like here.'

'Yes, so you keep saying, Sarge, but with all due respect, this is not Roxham, is it? I do think we should check it out.'

'If you insist,' sighed Barnett. He gave a laugh that sounded forced. 'The enthusiasm of youth, eh?'

It seemed to the listening man that there was an edge to the sergeant's voice now. Irritation? No, he thought, more than irritation. The man knew about Barnett, knew that he did not like being crossed. Knew how vindictive he could be. The man did not like Roger Barnett. Had not liked him ever since the officer had returned to the valley the previous year.

'Is that petrol?' asked the young constable, sniffing the air as the officers approached the pavilion.

'Might be,' said Barnett grudgingly. He walked over to the pavilion and knelt down to examine the petrol seeping across its wooden deck. 'Bloody kids. Why won't they leave the place alone? No respect, that's what it is. The younger generation has no respect.'

'Not all of them,' said the constable, walking to where the teenagers had been standing. She flicked a cider can across the path with her foot.

'Pissed up as usual,' grunted Barnett, hearing the sound and joining her. He reached down to pick up a cigarette tab. 'At least we know how they were going to set fire to the place.'

'You want me to go after them?' asked the constable, glancing towards the park entrance. 'I may be able to catch ...'

'Nah, they'll be long gone. Let's just leg it.'

'What if Harris...?'

'You leave Percy the Park Keeper to me, pet. I've got a big day tomorrow and the last thing I want is a late finish.'

The constable considered protesting but something in

Barnett's comment persuaded her to hold her silence. As the officers walked out of the park, the man peered over the churchyard wall, glanced at the pavilion, decided it was too risky and headed off into the night.

CHAPTER TWO

'And so,' said the grey-haired coroner, peering over his spectacles, 'I must bring this inquest to a close. I appreciate not everyone will agree with what I am about to say.'

All eyes turned to a tousle-haired woman sitting in the public area of the wood-panelled courtroom. She clutched a handkerchief on her lap and stared back at him out of a pinched face.

'However,' continued Henry Maitlin, 'my office dictates that I set aside the controversy that this case has engendered and deal only in facts. To that end, I am greatly obliged to the police for the help they have afforded me in this inquiry. This case has not been easy for them and I feel I must say that they have been subjected to undue pressure from some quarters.'

He glanced further along the wooden bench to where sat two plain-clothed officers: Jack Harris, strong jawed, thick brown hair without a hint of grey, and next to him Matty Gallagher, a decade younger, smaller, stocky, black hair starting to thin, a man with the appearance, colleagues often said, of a monk. Neither detective acknowledged the woman; they had not done so throughout the three hours of the hearing.

'But,' said Maitlin, 'I have to come back to the facts. Facts, ladies and gentlemen, have always been my bedfellows as I have attempted to execute my sworn duty as the coroner for this area. They have shone a guiding light into the very darkest of corners and have been my constant companions on the road I must tread.'

'Fucking hell,' murmured Harris in a voice so low that only the sergeant could hear.

Despite the gravity of the circumstances, Gallagher tried desperately not to laugh, pretending instead to cough. Several people turned to look and the sergeant tried to appear apologetic, difficult when he was aware of the sly smile emanating from the inspector.

'I have listened to the testimony given by Detective Sergeant Gallagher,' said Maitlin as the officer attempted to appear solemn, 'and noted his belief that Philip Morritt met his death following a fall. The sergeant's inquiries have been most professional and brought forth no evidence to support Mrs Morritt's hypothesis that her son died as the result of an assault.'

The woman glanced along the row towards Gallagher. Feeling her eyes boring into him, the sergeant did not return the look, instead allowing his gaze to stray up to the sharp November sun streaming in through the high windows in Levton Bridge's courthouse. During his previous career with the Metropolitan Police, Gallagher had been laid back about giving evidence but since his reluctant move to Levton Bridge, to allow his wife to be near her family, he had found formal hearings an ordeal, largely because everyone seemed to feel they had a right to share their pet theories with him. The run-up to Philip Morritt's inquest had been particularly testing with people regularly stopping him in the street to ask him his views on the case, probing him for scraps of information to feed into the rumour mill and expressing their disappointment when the sergeant declined to join in with their game.

'I also listened to the evidence given by Sergeant Roger

Barnett,' said Henry Maitlin, glancing at the uniformed officer sitting on the row to the left of the detectives. 'You will recall that he was the first policeman on the scene after Mr Morritt was discovered. Sergeant Barnett is a hugely experienced officer, a point he stressed to this hearing, and he supports DS Gallagher's belief that there was nothing suspicious about the death of this young man. I am aware there has been a suggestion of collusion between these officers but I find nothing to support that contention. Indeed, I find the suggestion vexatious.'

Philip Morritt's mother made a small sound but said nothing, her gaze locked on the coroner. I know that stare, thought Gallagher bleakly. Oh, how I know that stare. The sergeant switched his attention to Barnett, who had a smug expression on his face. Hearing Gallagher's sigh, Harris gave his colleague the merest of winks. Somehow it made Matty Gallagher feel better. You did not often get such gestures from Jack Harris but when you did …

'I have also taken evidence from a Leonard Portland,' continued the coroner, glancing at an unshaven man sitting on one of the benches, 'who, on the night in question, was drinking with Mr Morritt in several town-centre public houses. I know some people have questioned Mr Portland's power of recall….'

There were a few low laughs in the courtroom.

'Might I remind you,' said the coroner tartly, 'that this is a court of the land and, as such, requires respect.'

The laughter died away.

'Thank you,' said the coroner. He glanced down at his notes. 'Mr Morritt, you will remember from Mr Portland's testimony, indicated at the end of the night that he intended to walk to his home in the village of Chapel Hill, a distance of some two and a half miles. Given his state of mind on the night in question, and what we may call his colourful background, some people might doubt Mr Portland's testimony but, on this occasion, I found myself convinced by it.'

'That Levton Bridge then, Dave?' asked the passenger as the dark saloon car came to a halt on the crest of the hill. The two men looked across the moorland to slate-grey buildings and a church spire poking through the bare branches of trees.

'Yeah, that's it.' The driver, a thin-faced man with lank black hair, nodded. 'Chapel Hill's a couple of miles the other side, apparently. On the main road through the valley.'

'We sure about this?' asked the passenger as Dave started the vehicle moving again. 'I mean, really sure?'

'You getting cold feet, Ronny?' asked the driver, glancing at his travelling companion, a burly man in sweater and jeans. 'The last thing we want is another ...'

'Nah. Nah, I'm fine,' said the passenger quickly. 'You can count on me, Dave. It's just that it feels like we're taking a big risk on this one. I mean, if it's a small village there's more chance of someone seeing us and calling the cops. If Jack Harris ...'

'I told you, forget Harris. He's a backwater cop these days. More interested in sheep.'

'Yeah, but ...'

'Think of the money, Ronny. Yer man reckons it'll fetch fifty grand and we're down for ten of that between us. Think of that instead of worrying about some washed-up copper.'

'Yeah, I guess so.' The passenger nodded but he still looked uneasy.

Silence settled on the car once more as it began to drop down from the moor. Ronny's next words were spoken quietly.

'What happens if he disturbs us, Dave?' he said. 'I mean, when we're in there? How far do we go to get it?'

The driver did not reply.

*

Henry Maitlin turned his attention to another man sitting in Levton Bridge's courtroom. Thin faced, brown haired and wearing a smart black suit, the man's body language suggested impatience and he was glancing at his watch when the coroner looked at him.

'You also heard Robert Mackey give evidence,' said the coroner. 'Mr Mackey, as you will recall, lives in Laurel House, halfway between Levton Bridge and Chapel Hill. He recounted how, when he came out of his home the following morning, he discovered Mr Morritt on the roadside, the amount of snow about his person suggesting that he had lain there for a number of hours. Mr Mackey immediately called for an ambulance but by the time Mr Morritt reached Roxham General Hospital he was dead. Mr Mackey has also been subjected to attacks on his integrity. In my view, neither he nor any of the other witnesses have done anything to deserve such sleights on their character, slurs which can prove deeply divisive in such a tight-knit community as ours and whose impact cannot be overestimated.'

Rob Mackey inclined his head slightly in the direction of the coroner. Harris gave Gallagher a knowing look. The detective sergeant sighed again; the bastard will be insufferable now, he thought gloomily.

'So,' said the coroner, 'to my conclusions. Let me take you back to a country road late on a February night, the surface already icy, some would say treacherous, after several days of sub-zero temperatures....'

The man stumbled in the darkness and pitched forward. He did not feel what had hit him; at first he did not even know that he had been hit. Mind reeling, confused images swirling before his eyes, he sunk to his knees. He slowly turned his

15

head, trying desperately to focus on the spinning world around him, trying to make sense of what had happened. Vision blurred, body now racked with jagged pain, he tried to stand up but his legs buckled and he staggered forward once more, this time to lie still and silent on the cold ground. Looking up, he saw a face staring down at him and heard a voice echoing as if from afar. The voice fell silent and the face receded into the distance as the darkness closed in. The man was alone and he felt cold. He knew in that moment that he was dying. After that, he saw nothing, heard nothing, felt nothing. His was to sleep for ever. It was down to others to honour his memory.

'So,' said the coroner, 'all the evidence confirms that Mr Morritt had consumed a considerable amount of alcohol that night and there is no doubt in my mind that in his inebriated state, he slipped and fell, striking his head on the ground and sustaining the injury that was eventually to prove fatal.'

The coroner paused for dramatic effect. Gallagher stared up at the window again, Esther Morritt dabbed her eyes with the handkerchief and Rob Mackey glanced at his watch.

'God, he does milk it,' murmured Harris.

One or two people glanced at the chief inspector and Gallagher gave a little shake of the head without realizing he had done it. Despite having worked with the inspector for almost two years, he still struggled with his ways.

'I find then,' said Henry Maitlin, 'that I must return a verdict of misadventure and I so do. I thank you for your attendance. This hearing is at an end.'

'Thank God for that,' said Harris quietly to his sergeant. 'Man gets pissed and falls over. How long does it take to work that one out?'

There was a general murmuring as people started to stand up. Rob Mackey walked swiftly from the room.

'He's got the right idea,' said Harris. 'Come on, Matty lad, let's get out of here before the barn-pot woman collars us.'

Gallagher nodded and, as the officers pushed their way through the people and out into the corridor, he glanced back to see Philip Morritt's mother remonstrating with the coroner. The sergeant followed Harris out into the market place. Ignoring the waiting television camera crew, the detectives sidled along the side of the building and walked briskly past the row of shops and tearooms. As they turned the corner, a black saloon headed down the hill. The detectives watched it pass the Victorian house that had served as Levton Bridge's police station for as long as anyone could remember. When the car reached the crossroads, it slowed with just one brake light showing then turned right onto the road which led out of town.

'By, I'm glad that hearing's over,' said Gallagher. 'What do you make of what happened back there?'

'I told you how it would go. It was the only verdict the old buffer could possibly have brought in. He always does as he's told, does Henry. Not sure he needed three hours to do it, mind.'

'Can't disagree with that.' Gallagher glanced round and groaned as Esther Morritt appeared, walking swiftly towards them with a determined expression on her face. 'Not that everyone will agree, mind.'

'Her kind never do.'

'She's just upset, I guess. Maybe she will calm down now that the inquest has ...'

'Sergeant Gallagher!' shouted Esther Morritt.

'Yeah, perhaps you're right,' said Harris slyly as the detectives stopped walking. 'That sounds like a woman who has rediscovered her sense of perspective.'

Gallagher shot him a pained look then turned back to face the furious woman.

'Esther ...'

'Don't you Esther me,' she said, jabbing a finger at the

sergeant. 'What went on in there was a disgrace. An absolute dis—'

'We have been over this a thousand times,' said Gallagher wearily. 'Like the coroner said, we have to …'

'You're all in it together. I'm not stupid.' Now she jabbed a finger at the inspector. 'And you, you should know better than to let a man like this investigate what happened to my son.'

'A man like what?' asked Harris innocently.

'He doesn't understand our ways. Neither does that man Barnett.'

'Oh, come on, Esther,' said the inspector, in the kind of voice he would normally reserve for a small child, assuming that he was minded to talk to one, and he never was, 'DC Gallagher is a perfectly competent officer and Roger Barnett's from Roxham, for God's sake. Like it or not, this inquiry was conducted properly.'

'Rubbish! My son had just joined the army. Why would he throw it all away?' She turned on her heel and stalked back towards the market place. 'This is not over. Not by a long chalk.'

'Bloody small-town mentality!' exclaimed Gallagher when she was out of earshot and the officers had started walking again. 'It's not as if London is the end of the world! Besides, I live in Roxham as well, for God's sake!'

Harris listened with amusement. Although the sergeant's attitude to the valley could be irritating at times, the inspector could not help but agree. It was the claustrophobic nature of small-town mentality that had driven a teenage Jack Harris from the valley in the first place, and it was what made him think twice about coming back two decades later.

'And what's more …' continued Gallagher as the officers reached the police station.

They climbed the stairs to the first floor where Gallagher

turned right towards to the CID squad room, still chuntering, and a grinning Harris went left to his office where his dogs leapt to their feet and bounded across the room, tails wagging furiously. Harris beamed at the reception from Scoot the black Labrador and the detective's more recent acquisition from the local animal sanctuary, a scruffy Collie by the name of Archie. Never a great one for people, the inspector loved dogs. He also loved the fact that Philip Curtis tried to ban him from taking them into the police station when he first became divisional commander, only to be forced by staff protests to reverse the decision.

Having glanced at the reports on his desk, the inspector was about to replace the documents when something caught his attention and he peered closer. Study completed, Jack Harris headed out into the corridor.

CHAPTER THREE

Having pointedly refused to acknowledge the journalists gathered outside Levton Bridge court house, Rob Mackey went home after the inquest, edging his Range Rover up the tree-lined drive, tyres crunching on the gravel. Having parked outside Laurel House and cut the engine, he sat for a few moments, acutely conscious that his palms were sweaty and his heart was racing. Something, he assumed it to be fear, told him that this would be the day. After all, there was no way it could have stayed a secret for ever. Calming down, he tried to rationalize the situation. Perhaps he had got away with it, after all. He had been very careful; they both had.

Feeling slightly better, and with his heart-rate slowing, Rob Mackey got out and walked over to the house. Unlocking the front door – his wife was at work and his eighteen-year-old daughter at college in Roxham – he stooped to pick up the post from the doormat. Flicking through the bills, he stopped when he reached a white envelope. Rob Mackey knew what was in it. Waiting for its arrival had become a way of life and he had grown accustomed to the sharp twisting in his stomach every time he heard the postman's boots crunching on the gravel. And yet in a strange way, and one Rob Mackey did not understand, he wanted to savour the moment so he turned the envelope over and over in his hands. No, he thought, as he walked slowly through to the kitchen, savour was not the right word. He was not sure how to describe the feeling as he flicked the switch on the kettle, sat down at the table and stared at the envelope, which he had propped up against the toast rack. Perhaps the sensation he was experiencing was relief. Yes, perhaps that was it. Relief that the waiting was over.

After a few moments, he reached for the paper knife and slit open the envelope with exaggerated care. Out dropped a piece of paper. Mackey picked it up off the table and scanned it.

'And so it begins,' he said softly. He walked over to the boiling kettle. 'Or finishes.'

Followed by his dogs, Jack Harris strode along to the CID room where Matty Gallagher was standing by the window, watching the television crew approaching the police station. The sergeant noted that light rain had started to fall and was glistening on the camera. Next to him stood Alison Butterfield, a young blonde detective constable in a smart black suit.

'Matty reckons it was a bit tasty at the inquest,' said Butterfield as the inspector walked into the room. She reached down to stroke the dogs as they milled around her legs. 'Esther Morritt going off on one again.'

'As predicted,' said Harris, sitting down at one of the desks, the chair creaking under his weight.

'She had a go at me earlier this week,' said Butterfield, nodding.

'She's had a go at everyone,' commented Gallagher gloomily, still looking down into the street. 'Telly look like they want a chat about it, guv. That reporter bird, Landy or whatever she's called, she's with them. They're on the front steps. You going to talk to them?'

'I told Curtis to do it.'

'Told?' said Gallagher, raising an eyebrow.

'Suggested that it was more suited to his interpersonal communications skills,' said Harris with the ghost of a smile. He tipped back in the chair, placed his feet on the desk and glanced at Butterfield. 'All quiet then?'

'Some old dear got her handbag lifted from the Co-op. Not sure if we'll get it back. Or if it's lost in the first place. Nobody remembers anything happening and the staff don't reckon any of our locals have been in. Lenny Portland was at the inquest so that rules him out. It'll probably turn up on her kitchen table.'

'You're probably right. That all?'

'Traffic reckon all they've done is ticketed some guy for driving with a tail light out. Got him just as he came into town on the moor road.'

'Yeah, we saw him. Anything else?'

'Sir?'

'Anything off the overnight log?'

'No. Dead as the proverbial.'

Matty Gallagher turned his attention away from the television crew and to the conversation, marvelling, as usual, at the way Butterfield failed to read the signs with the inspector. The sergeant wondered whether to intervene – he had, after all, seen the entry on the log as well and realized that Harris would ask about it. Gallagher decided against it. The girl had to learn sometime. Besides, this was more fun.

'The British Legion bowls pavilion?' said Harris, an edge to his voice. 'Someone tried to set fire to it last night.'

'Oh, yeah, that.' The constable's tone was dismissive.

Gallagher closed his eyes. They never learn, he thought.

'Is that all you can say?' asked Harris.

'I talked to Katie Jarvis about. She reckons it was kids. There's always teenagers mucking about in the park. She and Roger Barnett found some empty cider cans.'

'And if it wasn't kids?'

'Roger Barnett reckons—'

'Roger Barnett,' snorted Harris. 'How many times have I told you about Roger Barnett? Right, since you reckon it's so quiet, you can accompany me to Chapel Hill.'

'What, for that memorial ceremony?' protested Butterfield. It felt like a punishment; she was just not sure for what. 'Do I have to?'

'Call it your civic duty. I'll meet you out the front when Curtis has finished boring the arse off the telly guys.'

Butterfield waited for the inspector and his dogs to leave the room then scowled.

'And don't look like that,' said the DCI's voice from the corridor. 'It's not becoming for a young woman.'

'How does he know?' asked Butterfield, looking at Gallagher. 'I mean, how the hell does he know?'

'Yeah, you're normally so enthusiastic about these kind of things,' said Gallagher. 'Surely the fact that someone had tried to torch the British Legion pavilion set some kind of alarm bells ringing, for God's sake? You've heard him banging on for the past few weeks. He's talked about nothing else. He's driving the girls in control bonkers.'

Butterfield shrugged, gathered her belongings and left the room.

'Will she never learn?' said Gallagher. He turned round to the empty office. 'Jesus, talking to myself now.'

Resuming his survey of events at the front of the police station, he watched as the uniformed figure of Superintendent Curtis walked down the steps. From his vantage point, the sergeant could see the drizzle glistening on the commander's balding head. Him and me both, Gallagher thought; must be the stress of working with Jack Harris. The sergeant noticed Curtis frown as he saw the inspector's white Land Rover parked by the front door. Everyone in the station had lost count of the number of times the commander had issued memos ordering staff to park in the yard. Harris had ignored them all, arguing that he'd always parked at the front and nothing was going to change that. Not even Philip Curtis. Especially not Philip Curtis. Gallagher grinned at the commander's irritation but quickly wiped the smile from his face as the superintendent looked up at the CID office window. Ducking back into the room, Gallagher chuckled. Sometimes, small-town mentality could be fun, he thought. Only sometimes, mind.

As he returned to his desk, the sergeant's mobile rang. He glanced down at the name on the screen. Harris.

'Now I wonder what he wants?' murmured the sergeant, taking the call.

'Got a little job for you, Matty lad,' said the inspector. 'Constable Butterfield might not think it's important but I want you to find out everything we know about the attempted arson on the British Legion pavilion last night.'

'Ahead of you but not really sure there's much more to tell.'

'Well, check again.'

'Yes, but ...'

'Humour me,' said the inspector and the phone went dead.

The drizzle had started to fall in Chapel Hill as well when the black saloon car entered the village and came to a halt alongside the green. For a few moments, the two occupants surveyed the bandy-legged man in overalls who balanced precariously on a stepladder as he rearranged the blue covering over the stone war memorial. The driver perused the rest of the village, his eyes taking in every detail. Like so many of the communities strung out along the main road through the valley, Chapel Hill was small, its slate-grey cottages crammed into half a dozen terraced streets, each one of which gave way to steep, wooded slopes. Many of the houses had a tired appearance and there had once been a corner shop but it had long since been boarded up, as had the derelict Methodist chapel at the top of the village.

'What a dump,' said the driver.

'Which one is it, Dave?'

'Halfway up.' The driver gestured to the street on the southern edge of the village. 'The one with the blue door, apparently.'

'We definitely doing it tonight then?' Ronny nodded at the man working on the memorial then at the bunting strung across the streets. 'I mean, what with all this going off and the—'

'We do it tonight.' The driver's voice brooked no argument. Noticing his accomplice's anxious expression, his demeanour softened. 'Will you stop worrying about it, Ronny. They're all old gadgies live here, they'll all be in bed with a mug of Horlicks by eight after all this excitement. Besides, yer man wants it as quick as possible.'

'I guess,' said Ronny, but he did not sound convinced.

The driver glanced in his rear-view mirror as a vehicle emerged round a bend at the top of the hill, followed by two more, all of which started to make their way down into the village.

'Time to make ourselves scarce,' he said and slipped the car into gear.

Having left the village and parked in the lay-by above Chapel Hill, the two men got out of the vehicle and looked back down towards the houses. The driver reached onto the back seat and produced binoculars through which he surveyed with interest the cars pulling up and the people beginning to assemble on the green, many of them white-haired men in blazers adorned by strings of medals.

'Honouring their dead,' he said. 'How appropriate.'

25

CHAPTER FOUR

It was shortly before one when Jack Harris emerged from the reception interview room where he had taken refuge while he waited for Curtis to conclude his press conference on the front steps. As the commander had fielded the journalists' questions, Harris had sat with his feet on the desk and his eyes closed, a faint smile playing on his lips. The dogs lay under the table. When the inspector heard the conference come to an end, he swung his legs down, walked over to the door and opened it slightly, peering cautiously out into the reception area. The grey-haired officer behind the counter noticed him.

'Don't worry, Hawk, he's gone,' he said. 'You in his bad books again?'

'Usually am, Des,' said Harris, slipping on his Barbour jacket and gesturing for the dogs to wait for him at the front door. 'Which way did his highness go?'

'Upstairs. Looking for you, I think.'

'Time to go in the other direction then,' said Harris and walked towards the door.

'Not trying to avoid me, I hope,' said a voice.

The inspector sighed and turned to see the commander heading back down the stairs.

'Of course not,' said Harris. 'As if I would. How can I help, sir?'

'I was just checking you were OK for the ceremony?'

'Just on my way there now. Will that be all, sir?'

Curtis looked irritated; he hated it when Harris pretended to be deferential. Both men knew that the inspector did not mean it. In many ways, Curtis preferred the bad-tempered version of the detective.

'Just behave yourself,' grunted the commander. 'Henry Maitlin asked for you specially, remember. You and Rob Mackey may not get on but just bear in mind that this is no time for antag—'

'Yes, well, I'll remember that. Excellent advice, sir,' said Harris, glancing at his watch. 'Gosh, is that the time? Got to be off. Don't want to be late.'

Curtis glowered as the inspector headed out of the front door, dogs following in his wake. The commander noticed Des Lomax grinning from behind the counter, scowled and walked back up the stairs, at the top of which he was almost sent flying by a rushing Alison Butterfield.

'Watch where you're going, young lady!' exclaimed Curtis, grabbing for the handrail.

'Yes, sir, sorry, sir,' said the constable and walked down the remainder of the steps.

Lomax grinned as she quickened her stride once she was in the reception area.

'How's the love life, young 'un?' he asked.

'None of your business,' she retorted as she struggled into her coat; they always had the same exchange.

'I'm always available, you know.'

'In your dreams,' said Butterfield, heading for the front door. 'Besides, I'm going out with someone.'

'Really?' Lomax looked at her with interest. 'A rival, eh? Anyone I know?'

'Like I said, it's none of your business.' Butterfield turned and pointed a finger at him. 'And I don't expect this to go round the station, right?'

The officer gave her his best innocent look as she

disappeared out of the front door and down the steps. Who, he thought, as he picked up the phone, should he tell first?

Jack Harris had already backed the Land Rover onto the road when Butterfield appeared. Once she had clambered into the passenger seat, he guided the vehicle through Levton Bridge's outskirts and out onto the valley road, the town's narrow streets soon giving way to dry-stone walls and steep wooded slopes.

'No need to look like that,' said Harris, as Butterfield sat in gloomy silence beside him. 'You might find this afternoon an education.'

'About what? I know you're into this kind of thing but they don't really do it for me.' Butterfield realized how it must have sounded so added quickly, in what she hoped was a more respectful tone, 'I mean, I know we should honour their sacrifice and all that but ...' Her voice tailed off. It just sounded lame.

'How many times have I told you to think these things through?'

'I said that we should respect their sacrifice and what they did for ...'

'This isn't about honouring a bunch of dead soldiers, Constable.'

'It isn't?'

'There's a lot more going on.'

'There is?'

'Certainly things a good detective should be aware of.' Noticing her bemused expression, he sighed. 'What do I keep saying, Constable?'

Butterfield thought for a few moments. 'Always read the situation?' she hazarded.

'Exactly.'

'But what's to read?'

'There's always something, Constable. What do we know about this afternoon?'

'Just that it's the unveiling of a war memorial.'

'A good detective never uses the word just. What else?'

'That Rob Mackey paid for it in memory of his father.'

'Well, in theory, it's in memory of all the Chapel Hill villagers who fell in battle but I imagine our dear Robert would much prefer your interpretation.'

'Wouldn't have thought there'd be that many of them to commemorate.'

'More than you might think,' said Harris, negotiating the Land Rover round a tight bend. 'Three from the Great War, two from the Second. Then, of course, there's Rob's father. I take it you know about the Mackeys?'

'I know you detest Rob.'

'That's besides the point.' Harris seemed irritated by the comment. 'What else?'

'Rob deals in antiques, doesn't he?' Butterfield trailed her hand over the back of the seat and Scoot and Archie competed for the chance to lick it first. She chuckled. 'Daft as a brush, both of them.'

'Yeah, they are,' said Harris, grinning, irritation momentarily banished. Now his voice was more even. Not friendly, though; Jack Harris's voice was rarely friendly. 'And Rob's father, what do you know about the venerated George?'

'That he was killed in the Falklands. The sarge reckons he was a hero.'

'Well, it rather depends if you believe in heroes but yes' – Harris nodded as the valley opened up to reveal the slate-grey roofs of Chapel Hill in the distance – 'yes, he was. He was a captain in the Paras who led his men on an assault on an Argentinian position above Port Stanley. Several of them were wounded but he kept going. Took it single-handed. Trouble was, another group of Argies heard the shooting and came rushing up the hill, all guns blazing. George fought them off as well but was hit in the stomach....'

The man stumbled in the darkness and pitched forward. He did not feel what had hit him, at first he did not even know that he had been hit. Mind reeling, confused images swirling before his eyes, he sunk to his knees. He slowly turned his head, trying desperately to focus on the spinning world around him, trying to make sense of what had happened. Vision blurred, body now racked with jagged pain, he tried to stand up but his legs buckled and he staggered forward once more, this time to lie still and silent on the cold ground. Looking up, he saw a face staring down at him and heard a voice echoing as if from afar. The voice fell silent and the face receded into the distance as the darkness closed in. The man was alone and he felt cold. He knew in that moment that he was dying. After that, he saw nothing, heard nothing, felt nothing. His was to sleep for ever. It was down to others to honour his memory.

'Did he die immediately?' asked Butterfield, trying to sound interested. Talk of military derring-do had never excited her imagination.

'Took him a day and half,' said Harris, slowing the vehicle to a halt to let a tractor edge past. 'I've seen a man die of a stomach wound. George Mackey must have been in agony. He was posthumously awarded the Military Cross.'

'Brave man.' It seemed the right thing to say.

Her disinterest in such matters had its roots in her upbringing as a farmer's daughter. Born and brought up in the valley, Alison Butterfield had never felt a strong connection with the military life. Her world, and that of her father and her grandfather, had always revolved around the Pennines' changing seasons. When the local newspaper ran the occasional story about lads in Afghanistan, it seemed too remote to be relevant. Even when a Levton Bridge man had been shot dead by insurgents in Helmand the year before, it had not really registered, although Butterfield remembered the coffin draped with a Union Jack being carried into the parish church for the funeral. Had she been moved by the scene? She tried to remember.

As Harris waved at the tractor driver and started the Land Rover moving again, a thought struck the constable.

'Did you win any medals?' she asked. 'I mean, when you were in the army?'

'The odd one.'

Butterfield waited for him to elaborate but he didn't. He never did. For a moment there was silence in the vehicle. It was broken by Harris.

'I take it you know that Rob Mackey tried to follow his father into the army?' he said. 'When he was a young man? Rejected on health grounds?'

'Is it relevant?'

'How many times do I have to tell you? Everything is relevant. You never know when these snippets of information will come in handy.'

'Right.'

Butterfield stared out of the window at the sheep grazing in the fields. Sometimes, she thought, sometimes she wished that she had taken up her father's offer to help run the farm. But not often.

'And because I do take notice,' continued Harris, 'I know that this afternoon is really all about Rob Mackey. He's an arrogant so-and-so. Just like his father.'

'But George was a war hero.'

'Doesn't make him a good man,' said Harris as the road started to dip towards the village and they saw a small group of people gathered round the memorial, still covered in its blue sheet. 'Nor is Rob for that matter. If you ask me, being rejected by the army hurt his pride. Today is the next best thing. Reflected glory.'

'Oh, come on,' protested Butterfield, 'that's a bit harsh, isn't it?'

'Is it? Is it really?' There was an edge to the inspector's

voice. 'Surely you must have noticed that George Mackey has more decorations than a bleeding Christmas tree? His name is already on the war memorial in Levton Bridge market place, there's a plaque on the library because he once borrowed a book there or something, there's one on their house, big thing with a military crest, and unless I am much mistaken, there's one on the pavilion in the park after Rob paid for its refurbishment. Now this.'

'Yes, but ...'

'What's more,' said Harris, bringing the Land Rover to a halt in the village car park, 'I happen to know that the parish council suggested Rob do the unveiling at the weekend. They thought Remembrance Sunday was the ideal time to do it but, no, he wanted it on its own. Wanted the limelight all to himself. And all for the sake of three days.'

'I bet he was hacked off when he heard it was the same day as the inquest then,' said Butterfield, unclipping her seat belt.

'The best laid plans, eh?' said Harris as he cut the engine. 'Pity about that.'

'Do you think Esther Morritt will turn up?' asked Butterfield as she got out of the vehicle and glanced towards the rows of cottages. 'She lives in the village, doesn't she?'

'Finally,' said Harris, gesturing for the dogs to remain in the back.

'Guv?'

'Finally you're thinking the thing through. The inquest is unlikely to have persuaded her that Rob Mackey did not kill her son. That's why they're here.' Harris nodded at the television van that had just pulled up alongside the van. 'Hoping that she puts on a show.'

'Ah.'

'Now those guys, on the other hand,' said the inspector, switching his attention to the elderly war veterans gathering on the green, 'you'd never hear them demanding a statue in their memory. Quite the opposite.'

'Right.'

'What's more,' said Harris, tossing his Barbour jacket into the back seat of the Land Rover and locking the vehicle, 'doesn't it strike you as odd that last night someone tried to torch the British Legion pavilion? I mean, ahead of today's events?'

'Uniform seem convinced that it was kids.' Butterfield caught sight of Barnett talking to a couple of veterans. 'Roger reckoned it was hardly even worth logging.'

'Roger always says it's kids. Means he doesn't have to do anything about it. However, that's the third time the place has been attacked. Windows smashed three weeks ago and someone tried to kick the door in two weeks before that. Jesus, am I the only one who thinks something weird is going on? Come on, let's get this over with.'

The inspector sighed; he hated ceremonies. Self-consciously, he tried to do up the top button of his shirt. It took him several seconds – Jack Harris was a big man – but eventually he managed it, wincing at the discomfort.

'Do I look OK?' he asked.

'You look lovely, guv.'

'Come on then,' grunted Harris. As he started walking towards the gathering, he noticed the scruffy figure of Lenny Portland loitering on the edge of the green. 'Not sure the presence of our local tea leaf fits in with Rob Mackey's world view. What's he doing here, I wonder?'

'Doesn't his aunt live in one of the cottages?'

'Yeah?'

'You never know when these snippets of information will come in handy.' Butterfield noticed his look with alarm and wondered if she had overstepped the mark. It was always difficult to predict how Jack Harris would react so she added quickly, 'Sorry, guv, er, sir.'

'I should think so,' said Harris but there was a twinkle in his eye. 'Cheeky basket.'

33

Butterfield laughed with relief. Harris gave the slightest of smiles; he loved the effect that his unpredictability had on people. The detectives walked over to the memorial where a bored-looking Rob Mackey was being engaged in conversation by Henry Maitlin, who had changed into grey slacks, a blazer on which were pinned several medals and a beret. Standing with them, Roger Barnett tried to appear interested in what the coroner had to say and greeted the arrival of the detectives with relief.

'Ah, Chief Inspector,' said Maitlin, 'I was just saying how fitting it is that a man of your background should represent the constabulary at such an occasion as this.'

'I guess it does seem appropriate,' said Harris as the men shook hands.

'I take it that awful woman won't be trying to disrupt this event as well?' said Mackey. He appeared irked by the inspector's presence and did not offer his hand to the detective.

'That awful woman,' said Harris, 'is a law to herself.'

'And there was me thinking that you were the law around here. It seems I was wrong.'

As Harris glowered at Mackey, Roger Barnett winked at Butterfield and the constable tried not to smile. The inspector could not pursue his conversation with Mackey further, however, because there was a murmuring in the crowd as everyone turned to survey an elderly man's slow procession down one of the streets, supported on the arm of a young dark-haired woman.

'If you want to talk about heroes,' said Harris to Butterfield, 'that's what one looks like.'

Still standing in the lay-by above Chapel Hill, the two men looked down on the gathering in the village. Noticing movement in one of the streets, the driver focused his binoculars on the white-haired man and the young woman walking slowly down one of the pavements.

'That's my boy,' he murmured.

'Leach?'

'I reckon so. Recognize him from that film.'

'Has he got it, Dave?' asked the passenger, reaching for the driver's binoculars. 'Has he got it with him?'

'Yeah, he's got it all right,' said the driver, producing a mobile phone from his pocket, dialling a number and lifting the device to his ear. 'You better still be interested.'

'I am,' said the voice on the other end. 'When you going to do it?'

'The village is pretty busy There's more people than we expected for this war memorial thing. And there's some bird with him.'

'Don't worry about her. She doesn't live with him. He'll be on his own tonight.'

'Nevertheless, maybe we should leave it for a day or two. Let things calm ...'

'My customer is most insistent, David. His buyer is due to fly out tomorrow night and he wants to take it with him.'

'Yes but ...'

'Just do it. If you can't, I'll get someone who can.'

The phone went dead.

'We doing it, Dave?' asked the accomplice.

'Yeah.' Before the driver could elaborate further, he noticed one of the figures on the green turn and look up towards them. He ducked beneath the wall. 'Get down.'

'What's wrong?'

'Harris.'

'Did he see us?' The accomplice sounded frightened as they hid behind the wall.

'Not sure.' Keeping low, the driver edged over to the car. 'Let's get out of here, Ronny. Last thing we want is that bastard snooping around.'

'Yeah,' agreed the accomplice, 'I've have had enough of Jack Harris to last me a lifetime.'

'What's wrong?' asked Butterfield, noticing Harris staring intently up at the valley road.

'Not sure. Thought I saw something.'

'I can't see anything,' said Butterfield, following his gaze.

'Must be my imagination. Maybe Esther Morritt has turned us all paranoid,' said Harris, turning back to the gathering. Hearing an engine start up, he turned again and watched the black car roof disappearing above the line of the dry-stone wall, adding thoughtfully, 'Or perhaps not.'

'I don't know much about medals,' said the constable, returning her attention to Harold Leach, who had reached the green to be surrounded by war veterans, 'but I know a Victoria Cross when I see one.'

'He won it in North Africa. Shot in the head but still managed to carry his sergeant a mile and a half to safety under heavy fire. God knows how they both survived. Didn't you see the documentary about him?'

'What documentary?'

'Channel 4 a few weeks ago. They told the story of four VC winners and Harold was one of them.'

'Who's the girl with him?'

'His granddaughter Maggie.' The gathering parted in respectful silence as the frail old man spotted Harris and walked over to the detective. The inspector extended a hand of welcome. 'Harold, how are you, my friend?'

It seemed to Butterfield that it was the first time in days that she had heard warmth in the inspector's voice.

'All the better for seeing you, Hawk,' beamed the veteran as they shook hands. Although his appearance was frail, the voice was strong and assured.

Butterfield stared at Harold Leach with fresh respect; everyone knew that only those very close to Jack Harris were permitted to call him Hawk. The female television reporter walked over to them.

'I wonder, Mr Leach,' she said, 'could we do an interview with you?'

'With me, my dear? Why on earth would you wish to do that?'

'To get your take on today's event.'

'I am sorry but this afternoon is about the men of Chapel Hill, not me.'

'Yes, but you live in the village as well,' said the girl, 'and you are the area's only VC winner. A real live war hero. And you did do that documentary. It's not as if you are a stranger to the camera, now, is it?'

'I can't help feeling that was a mistake,' said Harold unhappily.

'Nevertheless ...'

Harold glanced at Maggie for support.

'I don't think my grandfather feels it would be right,' said the granddaughter.

'Yes, but surely the—'

'Harold has made his views clear enough,' interrupted Jack Harris, stepping forward and fixing the television reporter with a stare. 'Don't you agree, Miss Landy?'

The reporter wondered whether or not to argue but something in the inspector's expression suggested it was a poor idea. She had had enough run-ins with Harris down the years to labour the point. All the journalists covering the area had similar tales to tell after bruising encounters with the inspector and she did not want to provoke a confrontation, certainly not at such a solemn occasion. And certainly not with Jack Harris.

'Of course,' she said and walked back to her colleagues, shaking her head at them.

Harold Leach murmured his appreciation to the inspector then moved over to talk to others.

'What was that about?' asked Barnett, walking up to Harris. 'Elaine Landy looks pretty naffed off.'

'That Harold does not wish to talk about his wartime experiences is a true measure of the man,' said the inspector.

'Rob Mackey seems keen enough,' said Barnett as he watched him warmly greeting the television crew.

'Also, I would suggest, a measure of the man.'

'For what is supposed to be such a proud occasion, there does not seem to be much goodwill around,' said Butterfield.

'That's what I have been trying to tell folks for weeks,' said Harris. 'Talking of goodwill, there's Barry Gough. I wondered if he'd turn up.'

A battered red Ford Escort had pulled up in the car park. When the driver emerged, it was a man in his early twenties, lank haired, sallow faced and wearing a scuffed parka. He reached into the back of the vehicle and produced a placard bearing, in scrawled large black letters, the words 'War is Wrong'.

'Do you want me to sort him out?' asked Butterfield.

'Yeah, go on. Oh, and do it before Mackey realizes that he's here. Tell him to sod off and protest somewhere else.'

'I'll try to find slightly more diplomatic phrasing, shall I?'

'That was the diplomatic version,' said Harris, watching her walk across the green towards the protestor.

Roger Barnett fell into step alongside her.

'Thought you might need a hand,' he said. 'Wouldn't be the first time we have had to move Barry on and he can get a bit spiky. A bit of experience can come in handy in these kind of situations, I always find.'

'I think I can cope.'

'I'm sure you can, pet.' He blocked Gough's way. 'I do hope you had not planned on disrupting this afternoon's ceremony, Barry.'

'It's a free country.'

'It's only free because of the sacrifice made by the men we are here to honour.'

'Rhetoric,' snorted Gough. 'You all spout the same garbage. That why the magistrate banned me from the market square this Sunday? If you ask me, some of these ...'

'Will you keep your voice down?' said Butterfield.

'I have every right to protest against the evils of war.'

A number of people shook their heads in disapproval and Butterfield noticed that Rob Mackey was now glaring balefully in their direction.

'Like I said it's a free ...' continued Gough but his voice tailed off as Barnett crouched by the front of the Escort and tapped one of the tyres. 'Here, what you doing?'

'Looks like the tread might be beneath the legal limit.' Barnett walked round to the other side of the car and made a big show of examining it. 'Ooh, this one's a bit iffy as well. Could cause a nasty accident, that could. I might have to seize the car, son.'

'You can't do that! You are just trying to ...'

'Of course, were you to get yourself off to Kwik Fit, I might be able to turn a blind eye to it this time.' Barnett gave him a mock-courteous smile. 'There's one in Levton Bridge. Behind the church.'

Gough opened his mouth as if to remonstrate but something in Barnett's expression made him change his mind and he stalked angrily back to the Escort.

'Bleeding disgrace,' he said in a loud voice as he got into the car and started the engine. 'It's a police state, that's what it is.'

'See,' said Barnett to Butterfield, as the officers watched him edge the vehicle out of the car park and drive out of the village, its driver still muttering angrily to himself, 'a bit of experience goes a long way. That was a little trick I learned down in Roxham. Got to know how to handle these kind of situations, Alison.'

Butterfield glowered at him but said nothing as they returned to the gathering just as Henry Maitlin began to speak.

'Ladies and gentlemen,' he said as he surveyed the brooding skies, 'I think we had better make a start. As chairman of the district branch of the British Legion, it is my privilege to welcome you to this solemn occasion. I am delighted to see so many of our military representatives present, including our dear friend Harold Leach. As I am sure many of you will know, Harold has not been well so it is a pleasure to see him up and about. This event is as much about those who are still with us as it is those who have departed. Is that not right, Rob?'

Maitlin glanced at Mackey, who nodded quickly in agreement when he noticed everyone staring at him. 'Ah, yes,' he said, 'yes, indeed, Henry.'

'Perhaps, given that the rain seems to be almost upon us, you would like to do the honours now, Rob? After all, without your generosity it would not have been possible.'

'Indeed so,' said Mackey, stepping forward and looking round the crowd. 'Some uncharitable people have suggested that I only provided the money for this memorial to honour my father but that is not the case. There are other names on this memorial. My father was proud of being born in Chapel Hill and often said it was a terrible oversight that it did not have its own memorial. I am delighted to put that right.'

Some among the gathering nodded in agreement and Mackey stretched out a hand to remove the covering, the blue material sliding smoothly down the side of the stone memorial to reveal the carved names beneath the words 'To Honour the Dead'. As the applause died away and people started to shake Mackey's hand, even Jack Harris looked impressed. The inspector's attention was distracted by a familiar figure stalking down one of the streets and onto the green.

'No show without Punch,' he murmured.

'Punch could be the word,' said Barnett. 'She's off her rocker, that one.'

Esther Morritt pushed her way angrily through the crowd and walked up to Rob Mackey. After reading the inscription on the memorial, she turned to him, fire in her eyes.

'Honour,' she said dismissively. 'What honour did my son receive? You tell me that, Rob?'

'I hardly think that this is the right time. Besides, I have said everything I want to say to you, you mad old bitch.'

'How dare you!' she exclaimed furiously then noticed the coroner standing next to Harris and Barnett. 'You're all in it together, the lot of you. You should all be ashamed of yourselves. My son was a soldier, just like your father, Rob, and he deserv—'

'Well, not quite like my father. My father died a hero in the service of his country.' Mackey gave her a sly look. 'Correct me if I'm wrong, Esther, but didn't your son get himself pissed up then fall over? The only courage he exhibited was the stuff he was throwing down his neck. Hardly likely to get the Military Cross for that, was he now?'

'How dare you say such things!' said Esther furiously, raising her hand.

'No you don't,' said Harris, gripping her arm.

Watching from a few feet away, Butterfield wondered if Esther Morritt would wrench her hand free and strike the inspector – and, as always happened when such incidents occurred, the constable wondered how her boss would respond if she did. Esther struggled for a few moments before lowering her hand.

'Just go home, love,' said Harris, his voice softer now. 'Please, Esther. It's for the best. Believe me, the last thing I want to do is arrest you. Not on a day like today.'

Esther looked at him for a few moments, glanced at the gathering watching the confrontation in silence and nodded meekly as the strength seemed to drain from her. She turned and walked wordlessly across the green, the crowd parting to let her through, the television crew following her with the cameraman filming her and Elaine Landy thrusting a microphone into her face.

'I want that woman arrested!' said Mackey furiously, deliberately loud enough and in Esther's direction. 'She's crazy! Off! Her! Head!'

He turned round but Jack Harris was already halfway towards the Land Rover and did not even acknowledge the comment as he strode across the grass. Butterfield glanced at Mackey, seemed about to say something then thought better of it, and followed her inspector to the vehicle. Watching them go, Roger Barnett walked over to stand next to Mackey.

'You need to watch your step, sunbeam,' said the sergeant in a low voice. 'The DCI would love nothing more than to arrest you.'

Rob Mackey said nothing as the Land Rover headed out of the village and the rain swept in low and hard across the valley.

CHAPTER FIVE

The rain had died away and darkness had long since deepened over the northern hills when the black car drove slowly back into Chapel Hill, the driver extinguishing its lights as it entered the village. Having parked up behind the bus shelter on the far side of the green, he and his accomplice got out and stood for a few moments, listening to the sounds of the night. More used to the city and its restless noises, they found themselves unnerved by a silence punctuated only by the plaintive sound of sheep high up on the hills and the distant hooting of a tawny owl in one of the copses that lined the valley.

'Let's get this done,' said the driver.

'If you're sure,' said Ronny.

'I'm sure.'

Without speaking further, the two men walked across the green, picking their way carefully through the darkness until they reached the street on the southern edge of the village and worked their way up along the tree-line at the rear of the cottages, illuminating their way with torches. Halfway up the slope, their feet slipping on the slicked grass, they hesitated as they heard the sound of Levton Bridge's town clock striking midnight, each mournful toll carried on the night air. Dave looked at the nearby cottage, which was shrouded in darkness.

'That the one?' whispered Ronny, noticing the gesture.

'Yeah, that's it. He must be asleep by now. Come on, let's risk it.'

The men clicked off their torches, climbed over the low wall and walked across the back garden. Once at the cottage, the passenger produced a jemmy and quietly, quickly, expertly, forced the back door allowing the men to enter the house. Hesitating for a few moments in the cramped kitchen, they listened for anything that might suggest that the occupant had detected their presence but all they heard was the settling of old timbers and a clock ticking on the living-room mantelpiece. They walked into the musty hallway. Upstairs, the old man stirred in bed and his eyes snapped open. For a few moments, he struggled to remember where he was or what had woken him. Hearing nothing, he closed his eyes again. Which was when he heard the creak on the stairs.

Out on the green, a figure emerged from the shadows and spent a few moments surveying the car behind the bus shelter before approaching the new war memorial.

Three hours later, with the village once more deserted, a door opened in one of the cottages and a man wearing a uniform stepped out on to the street. An employee of a delivery company, he was up early to drive down to Cheshire to pick up a package and bring it back to a bank in Roxham. He walked briskly down the street and across the green, illuminating his way with a flashlight. As he passed the war memorial, something glistened and he looked closer.

'Bloody kids,' he murmured with a shake of the head. 'There'll be hell to pay for that.'

He wondered whether or not to phone the police but a glance at the luminous dial of his watch made him decide against it; he was already on a tight deadline if the bank was to get its package by 9.30 a.m. The last thing he wanted was to be delayed making statements to the police. Feeling slightly guilty, but telling himself that someone else would report the vandalism, he walked across to his van in the village car park, fished his key fob from his pocket and unlocked the door. As he did so, he caught a glimpse of a figure on the far side of the green.

'Hey!' shouted the delivery driver but when he looked closer the figure had gone.

'Bloody imagination,' muttered the driver, tossing his lunch box into the passenger seat.

Within a few moments, his van was heading in the direction of Levton Bridge, its headlights carving a way through the night as peace returned once more to Chapel Hill.

CHAPTER SIX

Jack Harris had always believed that if you carried hell around within you, and he had plenty of reason to hold the statement to be correct, the same must surely be true of heaven. Not usually a man given to such whimsy, the inspector did experience occasional moments of reflection when away from his police duties and so it was that he found himself pondering the idea next morning as he stood at the summit of the hill. Surveying the misty moorland vista stretching away before him, dogs sitting at his feet and panting after their exertions, Harris was wrapped in silent contemplation as he appreciated his day off.

Taking the time owed to him from a protracted aggravated burglary inquiry the previous month had been a spur-of-the-moment decision the previous evening. After returning to Levton Bridge following the ceremony in Chapel Hill, the inspector had been summoned by Curtis. The divisional commander had just come back from a meeting with the chief constable at headquarters in Roxham at which had been outlined the need to cut overtime due to the force's financial difficulties. As the smallest force in England, money had always been a concern and all the senior officers realized that cutbacks were the preferable alternative to a merger with one of its larger neighbours. For that reason, Harris had offered only token resistance in the meeting with Curtis and returned to the CID squad room to announce that he would be taking the following day off.

Such freedom was the reason why Jack Harris had, some years earlier, left his post as a detective inspector with Greater Manchester Police to head north to Levton Bridge. Colleagues in Manchester had struggled to understand the reasoning behind his departure; everyone knew that, having joined GMP after a decade-long military career, Harris had been on the promotional fast-track, his superiors having identified his single-minded approach as something worth nurturing as long as his fiery temper could be kept in check. The decision to give it all up for a rural backwater astonished many and he soon grew weary of trying to explain it.

For the inspector's part, returning home had not been an easy decision either. He knew from his childhood that the valley was full of people like Esther Morritt with horizons narrowed by the hills that ringed their communities. Harris could understand why they felt like that; he had always cherished the isolating effect of the hills, eagerly grasping the opportunities they had afforded a young man out for adventure. As a teenager, he had spent many hours roaming the moors, always with a dog at his feet, scrabbling up scree slopes and traversing boggy land to pursue his passion for wildlife, spending hours watching the birds that survived in the unforgiving landscape, the ravens and the buzzards, the lapwings and the curlews. Eventually, reluctantly, the young Harris had acknowledged the need to explore beyond his own horizon and left the valley to travel the world with the Military. The hills had waited patiently for him, though, and when the time was right, had called him back. He always knew they would.

It was shortly before 9.30 and the inspector had been walking for the best part of two hours, having left home with the moors still shrouded in the final vestiges of night.

Home was a tumbledown cottage halfway up a nearby hill, largely obscured from the winding road below by a fold in the landscape. With light only just streaking the sky, he had ushered the dogs into the back of the Land Rover and edged the vehicle down the twisted path until it met the main road. After passing through Chapel Hill, not even casting a glance at the memorial, he had parked in a woodland clearing a mile from the village and set off to walk. Now, he stood and breathed in the sharp chill of the November morning.

Glancing to his left, he noticed the gable end of a large house poking through the treetops. He scowled. This was Laurel House and Harris did not wish his peace to be disturbed by thoughts of Rob Mackey, a man he had loathed like few others since an incident the previous year. As the force's part-time wildlife liaison officer, the inspector had been called in to investigate the shooting of a buzzard on a moor close to where Mackey bred pheasants. Harris had convinced himself that Mackey was responsible. The men exchanged angry words several times during the inquiry and Mackey lodged a complaint with the district commander. Curtis, as ever irked by the inspector's passion for wildlife at what the commander saw as the expense of more important investigations, demanded that his DCI call off the inquiry. The incident still rankled with Harris.

'Come on, boys,' said Harris with a click of the tongue to the dogs as he strode down the hill in the opposite direction to the house. 'We don't want him ruining our day out.'

As Jack Harris was turning his back on Laurel House, Rob Mackey was sitting in his kitchen, deep in thought as he nursed a cup of tea that had long since gone cold. His reverie was disturbed by the ringing of his mobile phone, which was lying on the table. For a few moments, Mackey watched the light on the screen but he did not reach out immediately.

Such exquisite torture, he thought, just like it had been with the letter. Wanting to know yet not wanting to know. And knowing anyway. After the phone had rung six times, he sighed and put the phone to his ear.

'We need to meet before I go back,' said the voice on the other end. 'There's something you need to know.'

Matty Gallagher stood in the middle of the green in Chapel Hill and stared bleakly at the defaced war memorial, the letters 'DIS' having been scrawled in bright red paint in front of the word 'Honour'.

'Harris will not like this,' said the sergeant gloomily. 'It's the last thing we need ahead of Remembrance Sunday.'

'I reckon you're right,' said Alison Butterfield, emerging from behind the memorial. 'There's nothing round the back, Sarge. Just the stuff on the front.'

'That's bad enough, isn't it?' The sergeant was about to comment further when a thought struck him and he gave her a sly look, vandalism temporarily forgotten. 'Hey, is it true that you have a new man in your life?'

'Can't a girl have any privacy around here?' The constable seemed genuinely irritated as she walked over to him. She lowered her voice even though they were alone on the green. 'I knew it was a mistake to tell Des Lomax. Might as well have put it on Twitter.'

'Didn't get it from Des. Not sure he even knows what Twitter is. No, I got it from one of the girls in the canteen. And she reckons she got it from Edith.'

'Jesus Christ, don't tell me that even the cleaner knows?'

''Fraid so, girl.' He gave her an impish look. 'Want to know where she got it from?'

Butterfield gave him a scathing look but said nothing.

'Going to tell me who this feller is, then?' asked Gallagher. 'Some rough-neck farmer? I hope he takes his wellies off before he sha—'

'Not that it is any of your business, but he's not a farmer, no. He's actually quite a civilized man.'

'So he does take his—'

'Oh, for fuck's sake, Matty, can we just concentrate on the job in hand?' snapped Butterfield.

'As you wish.' The sergeant held up his hand in mock surrender. It had been a welcome distraction from the vandalism but his expression clouded over as he looked again at the memorial. 'What a mess.'

'You going to ring him then?'

'I have this awful feeling that I may have to,' sighed the sergeant, glancing at his watch. 'Ten a.m. He's probably on top of a hill by now, making eyes at a lesser spotted something or other. Not sure he'll be best pleased about us ruining his day off.'

'Us?' said the constable, patting him on the shoulder and walking back towards the war memorial. 'You're the sergeant, you're the one ringing him.'

'Yeah, thanks for that.'

Hearing the sound of an engine, the sergeant turned to see a Range Rover pull up alongside the green and a furious Rob Mackey emerge from the driver's door and stride towards the memorial.

'Something tells me that this is going to be one of those days,' sighed Gallagher. 'Correction, another one of those days.'

By 10.15, Jack Harris and the dogs had dropped down onto the moor where, after walking for a few minutes, the inspector sat down on a rock and rummaged in his haversack for his flask of coffee and biscuits. The dogs sat in front of him, their eyes never leaving the packet of digestives. Harris flicked two biscuits through the air and watched the animals gulp them down.

'Greedy bastards,' he chuckled. His mobile phone rang. 'Jesus, can't a man get any peace?'

Harris fished the phone out of his Barbour jacket pocket and glanced down at the name on the screen. Gallagher.

'Matty, lad,' he said, 'this had better be important. And I mean really important because this is my day off and if you think ...'

'Someone has vandalized the new war memorial at Chapel Hill.'

'Vandalized? How?'

'Painted red letters over it so that it reads "Dishonour". Rob Mackey has already gone off on one. If you look up, you might just see him. He must be in orbit by now.'

'And there was me thinking it was a buzzard,' said Harris, glancing up at the leaden skies. 'Where are you now? In the village?'

'Yeah. Butterfield is using her womanly charms to persuade Mackey not to kick down Esther Morritt's door. I keep telling him it's more likely to be kids but he won't listen.'

'It's too specific for kids,' said Harris, tossing another couple of biscuits to the dogs. 'I mean, they didn't just slap the paint on, did they? There's a very pointed message in there, if you ask me. Got to be aimed at Mackey.'

'I guess so but it doesn't necessarily mean it's down to Esther, does it? Barry Gough was here yesterday, remember. Trying to waggle his placard about. According to Alison, he was really hacked off at the way he was kicked out of the village by Barnett.'

'He's a liability that man.'

'He certainly riled Barry Gough. And Gough is just the type of crackerjack to do something this stupid.'

'Not sure I would have said vandalism is his style,' said Harris, taking a gulp of coffee. 'Maybe you should have a quiet word with him, just to be sure, though. And Esther as well, for that matter. Be nice to think we could keep a lid on this.'

'Which is why I rang you. Wondered if you fancied talking to her? Sensitive case and all that. There'll be lots of media interest once word gets out and I'm hardly her favourite person at the moment so it might make more sense if ...'

'Good try, Matty lad,' said Harris, standing up, scrunching up the biscuit packet and thrusting it into his bag, 'but Esther Morritt is your problem. Call it a cultural exchange.'

'Thought you'd say that,' said the sergeant gloomily. 'Think of me while you're enjoying your hike then.'

'How many times? I am walking, not hiking. People in stupid bobble hats, they hike.'

'Yeah, whatever,' said Gallagher and the phone went dead.

'Bloody southerners,' murmured Harris, reaching down to screw the lid back onto his flask.

Having finished his conversation with the inspector, Gallagher walked over to the memorial to join Butterfield, who was standing a few yards from the memorial, watching Rob Mackey as he stared with a thunderous expression at the paint.

'You not calmed him down then?' said the sergeant in a low voice.

'Not sure he'll listen to anyone, the mood he's in. I just told him that you were in charge of the inquiry and that he should deal with you.'

'Now where have I heard that before?' murmured Gallagher.

The detectives' attempts to keep the situation low-key were looking increasingly forlorn as a number of villagers started to gather round to watch the altercation.

'I want that bloody woman arrested!' said Mackey loudly, turning and striding towards them. 'She's a lunatic!'

'That's no way to talk about the constable,' said Gallagher, hoping that the comment would ease the tension. It didn't.

'That woman is running a vendetta against me and all you can do is make jokes! You've done nothing to protect me from Esther Morritt's rantings and ravings! And this ... this ... ' Mackey gestured angrily at the memorial. 'This is an absolute disgrace.'

'I agree with you,' said Gallagher. 'I just don't think we should jump to conclusions.'

'Yeah, come to think of it I did see that little tosspot Barry Gough trying to disrupt things yesterday,' said Mackey, with a curl of the lip. 'Should have lamped the little toerag when I had the chance.'

'I heard you and he had a bust-up a couple of weeks ago. You do seem to have a remarkable gift for making friends, Mr Mackey.'

'Well, what do you expect me to do? Him and his little mates were in the market place with those stupid placards. I told them what I thought of them and Gough, he gives me some backchat.' Mackey looked at the memorial. 'Mind, I still reckon this is down to Esther Morritt. I take it you are going to arrest her?'

'We will have to ...'

'Because if you won't, I will.' Mackey gestured up to the street. 'I'll drag the crazy bitch down here by her hair.'

'Will you please let us handle it?' said Gallagher sternly, patience finally exhausted. 'We will go and have a chat with—'

'Chat ... chat! It needs more than a chat!' Mackey pointed at the memorial stone. 'Five and a half thousand quid that thing cost me! Five and a half thousand quid!'

'That's what they mean by a high price being paid,' murmured Gallagher, his voice so low that Mackey was unable to make out the words.

'What? What did you say?'

'Nothing.' Gallagher motioned for Butterfield to follow him across the green. Once the detectives were out of Mackey's earshot, the sergeant added, 'They're off their rockers. All of them.'

'That's rough-necks for you.'

'Yes, thank you, Constable,' said Gallagher, shooting her a pained look. 'Come on, let's get this over with before Rob Mackey bursts a blood vessel.'

Half-way up the street, the sergeant glanced through the front-room window of one of the cottages and tensed.

'Hello,' he said quietly.

'What's wrong?' asked Butterfield. She watched him walked over and peer through the grimy glass. 'What you seen?'

'I hate to think.'

Butterfield leaned forward to look over his shoulder, struggling to make anything out through the film of dirt. It took a few moments for her eyes to grow accustomed to the darkness of the room.

'That does not look good,' she said quietly when they did.

Gallagher tried the front door but found it locked so the detectives jogged up the street, past Esther Morritt's home and through the band of trees that took them round the top of the village and back down along the rear of the properties. Halfway down, they climbed over the low wall at the end of one of the gardens. Walking quickly up the path, they noticed that the back door had been forced.

'Definitely not good,' said the sergeant as the detectives stood for a few uneasy moments before he led the way into the cottage, through the narrow kitchen and into the gloomy hallway.

'Hello! Anyone in? It's the police!' shouted the sergeant but there was no answer. He gestured at Butterfield. 'Check the bedrooms, will you? I'll take a look in the living room. Oh, and be careful. I don't like the feel of this.'

As Butterfield headed quietly up the stairs, Matty Gallagher stood in the hall for a few moments, his heart pounding and his hands clammy. The sergeant had seen many scenarios like this during his time in London and already had a sick feeling in the pit of his stomach. Such scenes had something that he had never been able to describe. Not a smell. Not even a feeling. It was, he concluded as he stood there, something about the silence. A heavy, oppressive silence. For a moment he was back in a terraced house in London, his first murder inquiry as a young officer. That house had the same silence that he felt now.

'Bugger,' said Gallagher.

Having composed himself, he walked into the living room and surveyed the devastation: drawers wrenched out of the dresser and discarded on the carpet, seat cushions hurled onto the floor and an upturned table lying amid the shards of a shattered vase. The sergeant's gaze strayed to the photograph hanging on the wall. Gallagher stared into the face.

'Well, if you're going to pick a victim,' he sighed, 'you might as well pick a good one.'

'Guv,' came Butterfield's voice from upstairs. It sounded flat.

Gallagher knew what she had found.

Jack Harris shouldered his haversack, trying to blot out what he had just been told by his sergeant. It was not easy and as he walked across the soggy moor, his thoughts grew darker, his mind constantly wandering back to the attack on the war memorial. It would, he knew, only serve to increase the tension in the valley. He recalled a seminar on rural policing that he attended shortly after returning to Levton Bridge. The officer giving the talk, who had been based in a similar upland division to the inspector's, had said, 'Where do you think my fear of crime is highest?' One sergeant had said, 'The housing estates in your towns?' 'Wrong,' the officer had replied. 'They are used to crime, see it most days. Sounds callous, I know, but it's a fact of life, I am afraid. No, my biggest fear of crime is in my rural areas where nothing happens from one month to another.' Noticing the puzzled expression on some of the officers' faces, he had explained: 'Why? Because when someone nicks a quad bike from a farm, the shockwaves ripple through all the communities for weeks. And you can multiply that tenfold when, God forbid, you get a murder. The place goes into meltdown, take it from me.'

God forbid you get a murder. Those words resonated now with Harris. He stopped walking as a thought struck him. Had he erred? Had they already seen a murder but not recognized it for what it was? Had he blindly backed Gallagher against Esther Morritt without properly considering all the options? Had her son really been the victim of an assault that night? Had he...?

'No,' he said, 'Matty was spot on and there's an end to it.'

Harris glanced down at the dogs, who were eyeing him expectantly. The inspector cursed under his breath. He hated it when work impinged on his walks.

'Enough,' he said. 'We're supposed to be on a day off.'

Harris could not be sure but it seemed that Scoot nodded in agreement. The inspector chuckled and had just started to walk again when his mobile phone rang. He took the phone out of his pocket and looked at the screen. Gallagher, it said. Harris tensed.

'What now?' asked the inspector irritably into the phone. 'Can't you sort out a hot-head with a pot of paint without me?'

'It's not the graffiti that worries me,' said the sergeant's sombre voice. 'I am afraid we got us a murder.'

God forbid.

'Don't tell me that someone has killed Esther Morritt?'

'No such luck, guv.' Gallagher hesitated. 'Look, I'm sorry but I'm afraid the dead guy is your mate Harold Leach.'

Harris closed his eyes. 'Are you sure?' he asked.

'He's been done over good and proper. Didn't have a chance, poor fellow. You coming down?'

'I'm on my way.'

'Quick as you can. There's already quite a few media here – someone tipped them off about the vandalism – and they're asking what's happened at the cottage. That television reporter – Landy or whatever she's called – she's getting arsey about it.'

'I'll be as quick as I can,' said Harris, slipping his phone back into his pocket and looking down at his dogs.

'Sorry, boys,' he said. 'Duty calls.'

The driver eased the dark vehicle into a parking place at the motorway service station and cut the engine.

'What now?' asked his passenger.

'We wait.' The driver noticed his friend's worried expression. 'Don't worry about it, Ronny. There's no way they can trace it back to us. We were careful. You know that. And we never meant to ... I mean, the old bastard shouldn't have ...'

'But he did, didn't he, Dave? He did and we ...' He saw a man walking over to the car. 'That him?'

'That's him, and he ain't going to be happy about this. Not happy at all.' Dave wound down the window.

'You got it?' asked the new arrival.

'Yeah,' said Dave, reaching over to open the glove compartment and producing a small brown paper package. 'Look, there was a bit of a hitch.'

The man looked hard at him. 'Hitch?' he said. 'What kind of a hitch?'

'We just heard on the radio that the old guy is dead.'

'Dead?' The man leaned into the car and hissed, 'How the hell did that happen?'

'He was alive when we left him,' said Dave defensively.

'Well, he's not bloody alive now, is he?' The man got into

the back of the car and leaned forward. 'This changes everything. The thing will be red hot now. Every copper in the land will be after us.'

'Not backing out, are you?' said Dave, turning in his seat. 'Because we've taken a huge risk for you and if you are ...'

He did not finish the sentence but let the words hang in the heavy air inside the vehicle. Dave looked hard at the man, who appeared deep in thought.

'Well?' asked Dave after a few moments, holding up the package. 'Are you taking it?'

'Yeah,' said the man, reaching forward for the package and handing over an envelope. 'Yeah, I am. It'll be out of the country by tonight. But there'll be a lot of shit flying over this and if you even think of talking to Jack Harris and his people you know what it means for you.'

Dave tore open the envelope and looked at the bank notes.

'I understand,' he said.

'Be sure you do,' said the man, getting out of the car. 'You just be sure you do. Harris will be all over this like a rash.'

Jack Harris and Matty Gallagher stood in the half-light of Harold Leach's bedroom and stared in silence at the battered body lying on its back beside the bed. The old man's face was heavily bloodstained and his jaw looked as if it had been broken. His left arm was twisted at a grotesque angle and his pyjama jacket was ripped in several places.

'A fighter to the end,' said Harris quietly.

'No medals for this one, unfortunately.'

'No indeed,' said Harris. As he looked into the dead eyes of Harold Leach, the inspector shuddered, an unusual reaction for a man inured to murder. But then they were not usually friends.

'You all right?'

'Yeah.' Harris walked over to the window and peered through the curtains. Having gone home to change hurriedly into a suit before he headed for the village, the inspector reached into his pocket and produced a red tie which he proceeded to put on while he surveyed the scene below. 'So much for keeping things low key, eh?'

Gallagher joined him and for a few moments they stared down at the small crowd that had gathered outside the cottage. Butterfield and a uniformed constable were trying to keep order but without much success. Several people were crying and being comforted, others stood in grim-faced silence. On each face was etched the lines of shock. Harris

59

remembered those words during the seminar and knew how they felt. He felt the same. The effect of the killing would be experienced for a long time, he imagined. God knows where it would end up, he thought.

Gallagher watched the inspector struggling with his tie. I wonder, the sergeant asked himself, how long it will be before he says that he told us so? He helped his boss straighten his tie.

'Thank you,' said the inspector. 'All fingers and thumbs today.'

'You sure you're all right?'

'Yeah, just a bit shaken up, you know.' The inspector looked over to the body. 'Harold was a good friend. Someone I admired.'

'I know.'

'I knew something like this would happen.'

'I know that as well.'

Harris nodded. 'Yeah, I guess you do,' he said with a slight smile. 'I guess I have banged on about it.'

'Perhaps we should have shown more respect for your instincts.' Gallagher looked at the body. 'After all, poor Harold is dead, is he not?'

'He is indeed.' The inspector glanced back out of the window and craned his neck to see further down the street, where he noticed more people arriving, recognizing one of them as a local newspaper reporter who appeared to be interviewing Roger Barnett as they walked.

'Not sure Barnett agrees about keeping things low key,' said Gallagher. 'Another chance to get his name in the papers.'

'The sooner we get Harold out of the village the better. The last thing we want is a bloody media circus.'

'Might make more sense to get Roger Barnett out,' said Gallagher. 'Besides, not sure we can really avoid the media scrum. Dead war hero, brutal killing, the journos will absolutely love it. We had something similar when I was with the Met. Even had one of them trying to sneak in through the back of the house. Pretended to be the old guy's nephew when we collared him. It's such a noble profession.'

'You're probably right,' sighed Harris. His gaze settled on the scruffy figure of Lenny Portland, loitering on the edge of the crowd and staring up intently at the cottage.

Noticing the detective watching him, Portland turned and walked quickly down the street, past Roger Barnett and out of the inspector's view.

'Now why is he here, I wonder?' said Harris.

'What you seen?'

'Lenny Portland. Seems to keep turning up like the proverbial.'

'This is way out of his league.' The sergeant's attention switched to the blonde television reporter conducting an interview with Henry Maitlin further down the street. 'I hope they've got a lot of tape in that camera.'

Harris allowed himself a smile; as so often with the sergeant, his comment had eased the tension in the room.

'So what have we got?' he asked, turning back into the room. 'Anyone see or hear anything last night?'

'Neighbour heard some thuds around midnight.'

'They not investigate?'

'She's eighty-seven.'

'So?'

Gallagher was about to remonstrate with Harris but the inspector gave the slightest of smiles and the sergeant thought better of it; it was like he always said, you just never knew with the DCI.

'The thuds must have been loud, mind,' said the sergeant instead. 'The old dear's Mutt 'n' Jeff. Got to be robbery, hasn't it? Forensics still can't find his VC, and whoever did it left some of the other medals so it looks like they knew what they'd come for.'

61

'It's a high price for a bit of gun metal, Matty lad. You get to talk to Esther Morritt?'

'Came across this on my way to see her. I reckoned that a bit of vandalism paled into insignificance so I ...'

'Might be worth it all the same. There's been plenty going off in the last few days and a lot of it centres on Esther Morritt and her mouth.'

'Yeah, but surely they're unconnected?' Gallagher gestured to the old man. 'I mean ... this is much more...?'

'Can't assume anything,' said Harris, walking over to the door. 'We ought to talk to Barry Gough as well.'

'The anti-war guy?' Gallagher was unable to conceal his incredulity this time. 'That's even more crazy than thinking that Lenny Portland might have been—'

'Like I keep telling people,' said the inspector as he headed down the stairs, 'the way things have been going lately, anything is possible. Absolutely anything.'

'Within reason,' muttered Gallagher under his breath and followed him out of the room.

At the bottom of the stairs, the inspector walked into the living room and, after nodding at the forensics officers, looked at the picture of Harold Leach on the wall, medals pinned on his blazer, VC taking pride of place. Next to the picture were other framed photographs; Harold being introduced to the Queen at a royal garden party, Harold meeting the prime minister when he visited Levton Bridge, Harold with his grandchildren at a Christmas party. With a sigh, the DCI walked out into the hallway and into the street where he was confronted by the sight of Rob Mackey pushing his way through the crowd.

'I hope you're still going to talk to Esther Morritt,' said Mackey, jabbing a finger at the inspector.

Gallagher, following Harris out of the house, shook his head when he heard the comment. There were plenty of things guaranteed to evoke a reaction from Jack Harris —

most things, actually – but few bettered pointing a finger at him and demanding that he do something. What's more, the sergeant knew – everybody in the valley knew – that there was bad blood between Harris and Mackey. Gallagher knew that was why Harris had been happy for him to handle the Philip Morritt case. Said he couldn't trust himself to keep his temper with the man.

'I asked you a question,' said Mackey as Harris ignored him. 'You had better not forget what the bitch did to my memorial stone just because some old guy has been done over.'

People in the crowd looked at Harris, waiting for the reaction. They were not to be disappointed. Seeing that the inspector's fist was bunched, Gallagher held his breath and prepared to intervene.

'Some old bloke?' said the inspector. 'Is that what he is to you – some old bloke?'

'Yeah, well, it's very sad and all that,' said Mackey, the murmuring in the crowd making him realize that he had overstepped the mark, 'but it does not mean that you should ignore your duty to—'

'Do you know,' said the DCI, walking forward so that his face was within inches of Mackey's, 'I have had just about enough of your whining voice. In fact, if I never heard it again, it would be too soon.'

'Now hang on a minute, Harris....'

'So might I suggest that you sod off out of this village before I rearrange your face?' said Harris quietly.

Mackey stared in amazement at the inspector, looked as if he was about to retort but, on hearing the applause rippling round the gathering and noting the detective's thunderous expression, thought better of it. He turned on his heel and stalked back down the street, furiously rebutting the television reporter's attempts to interview him. Gallagher relaxed slightly. Harris noticed Butterfield staring at him.

'Well?' he said. 'You got something to say, Constable?'

Butterfield shook her head meekly. 'No, sir,' she said. 'Of course not.'

'Good,' said Harris, brushing past her and walking through the crowd, which parted respectfully to let him pass. 'Right answer.'

'It's what's called community policing,' said Gallagher helpfully to the young constable as he walked past her.

Butterfield smiled weakly then turned her attention back to the crowd, which was pushing closer to the cottage again.

'Come on, you lot,' she said. 'Step back.'

Gallagher caught up with Harris near the green. 'You still want me to go see Esther Morritt?' asked the sergeant, falling into step with the inspector.

'No,' said Harris with a half-smile, the irritation of a moment ago banished as quickly as it had flared. 'I would have said that it pales into insignificance given what's happened here. Wouldn't you agree, Matty lad?'

Gallagher nodded. Sometimes Jack Harris could be almost human, he thought. 'Couldn't have put it better myself,' he said.

'Indeed.'

As they stepped onto the green, Henry Maitlin approached them; the officers could see that he was fighting back the tears.

'A terrible business,' he said, voice trembling. 'And with Remembrance Sunday so close.'

'Tragic,' said Harris, nodding.

Maitlin looked at the inspector with moist eyes. 'Have you any idea who did this, Jack?' he asked. 'I mean, what had he ever done to harm anyone?'

'We think they were after his VC, Henry.'

'Medals can fetch a lot on the black market if you've got the right buyer,' said Gallagher.

'Disgusting,' said Maitlin and his voice was urgent now.

'You have got to get whoever did this quickly, Jack. You know what people round here are like.'

'I am afraid I do, Henry. What have you been hearing?'

'I've already had several old dears from the village coming up to me saying they are frightened to sleep in their own homes tonight.' Maitlin glanced across to where the young television reporter was watching as her cameraman filmed people heading into the street. 'And when she interviewed me, that Landy girl asked me if I thought Chapel Hill was a safe place to live. I did not know what to say, Jack.'

'Tell them they'll be safe enough. This place will have officers on patrol all night. I'll see to that.'

'I'm not sure that will be enough. Folks are really scared.'

'I'm sure it's a one-off.'

'I hope you're right.' Maitlin hesitated. 'Don't be too hard on Rob Mackey, Jack. I know you don't like the man but he's been very generous to the Legion. Even paid for the refurbishment of the pavilion. I don't know what we would have done without him.'

'I'll bear that in mind,' said Harris bleakly as Maitlin headed off towards the cottages. The inspector looked at Gallagher as the men started walking again. 'Do we really have nothing?'

'Pretty much. Forensics reckon the place is clean. Whoever did this knew what they were doing. This feels like pros, it really does, and that means they have got to have come from outside.'

'I guess you're right,' said Harris as they paused at the war memorial. He surveyed the graffiti then turned as Barnett approached. 'Give me some good news, Roger.'

'Might be able to do just that. That old bloke over there by the phone box, chap with the little dog? Well, he lives down the bottom of Tenter Street and reckons he was woken up by the sound of a car door sometime after midnight. Looked out of the bedroom window and saw a vehicle on the far side of the green. He says it disappeared towards Levton Bridge.'

'He get a good description?'

'His knowledge of cars stopped when the Morris Marina went out of production. However, he did notice that one of its brake lights was out.'

'The one we saw yesterday,' said Gallagher. 'Didn't Butterfield say that traffic had given it a ticket?'

'She did indeed,' said Harris as he headed off across the grass towards the car park. 'Get on it, will you?'

'Sure. Where will you be?'

'Got to talk to an old friend.'

Roger Barnett looked quizzically at Gallagher. 'An old friend?'

'Leckie,' said the detective sergeant, 'it'll be Leckie.'

'Chief Inspector!' called a woman as Harris reached his Land Rover.

The inspector turned to see the television reporter and her crew approaching.

'Ah, Miss Landy,' he said thinly, 'taking a break from scaring the shit out of innocent old people, are we?'

'I don't think that's a fair comment, Chief Inspector. After all, a man has been murdered here – can't exactly exaggerate that, can I? Oh, don't look like that, Jack, you know it's true. Everyone seems to believe that the dead man is Harold Leach. Can you confirm that?'

'We have not made a formal identification yet,' said Harris, giving her a hard look, 'but if it is him, that will be Harold Leach VC to you and me. Around here, young lady, we honour our dead. I suggest you do the same.'

'Not sure they honoured Harold.'

Harris said nothing, turned and walked over to his vehicle. Standing not far away, on the edge of the green, Lenny Portland was watching the confrontation when his mobile phone rang. He fished it out of his parka pocket.

'Yeah?' he said.

'It's me,' said a man's voice. 'You better not be responsible for what happened last night.'

'It weren't nothing to do with me. I wouldn't do a thing like that.'

'Well, someone did the old bastard over.'

'I tell yer, it weren't me that killed him. Got to go. Harris.'

Having unlocked the vehicle, the inspector had heard the phone ring and had turned to see Portland. Seeing the inspector walking towards him, Portland slipped the phone into his pocket and headed in the opposite direction.

'Lenny!' shouted the inspector.

Portland turned to face the detective and tried to sound calm.

'Morning, Mr Harris,' he said. 'How can I help you?'

'You can tell me what a tea-leaf like you is doing here for starters?'

'It's a free country.'

'Been listening to Barry Gough, have you?'

'Don't know the man.'

'So what are you doing in Chapel Hill, Lenny?'

'Visiting me aunt.'

'You and she must have a lot to talk about. That's two days running you've been here. I saw you at the unveiling yesterday as well. She teaching you embroidery, perhaps?'

Portland looked bemused.

'Never mind,' said Harris. 'You would not happen to know anything about what happened to Harold Leach, would you? Not got a sudden penchant for shiny things, have we?'

Portland's eyes widened. 'That ain't nothing to do with me. Honest, Mr Harris. You know it ain't my style.'

'Yeah, maybe you're right,' agreed Harris, 'but so help me, if I hear that you were tied up in this—'

'You won't, Mr Harris. Honest. I have too much respect—'

'Get out of my sight, Lenny.' Portland gave him a relieved

look but it faded with the inspector's next words. 'And I wouldn't look that cheerful. Constable Butterfield still wants to speak to you. About a handbag theft, oddly enough. In fact, there she is now.'

As Harris turned to watch the young constable approaching across the green, Portland seized his opportunity and scuttled over to the bus stop.

'What did Lenny want?' asked Butterfield, watching him go.

'Wanted to talk to me about civil liberties. I told him that he was in the frame for that handbag snatch. Have you got anywhere on that?'

'No. I thought that with what happened to …'

'Well, I want you to nick him for it.' Harris noticed Portland waiting at the bus stop. 'And I want you to do it now.'

'Now? Surely you don't think that he has anything to…?'

'Do you know,' said Harris irritably, 'every bastard seems keen to tell me who didn't murder poor old Harold Leach. Perhaps someone would like to tell me who did instead. Make a nice change, wouldn't it? Just lift Lenny Portland, will you?'

'Yes, sir. Of course, sir,' said Butterfield quickly.

She noticed with alarm that the bus had pulled up at the stop. The constable started to run towards the vehicle but Portland had already clambered aboard. The bus pulled away with him sitting at the back seat. He was on the phone.

'I just hope,' said Harris, glancing at the constable as the vehicle rumbled out of the village, 'that he's not talking to anyone important.'

'So do I,' said Butterfield. 'So do I.'

Rarely had she meant anything more.

CHAPTER EIGHT

Once in the Land Rover, Jack Harris reached onto the back seat to greet the dogs and was about to make the call when his mobile rang. He glanced down at the screen: Stuffed Shirt, it said. Harris sighed; better take it this time, he reckoned. He'd already missed three calls.

'Jack, that you?' asked Curtis.

'Yeah, it's me.'

'I have tried your mobile several times without answer,' said the district commander. 'Where have you been?'

'Bad reception.'

'That one again.' Both men knew that the inspector had been ignoring the calls. Always did. It had been a major bone of contention between them for years. 'I take it you are in the village now?'

'Yeah, been here for some time.'

'And?'

'And what?'

'And what have you found out?' said Curtis, the irritation clear in his voice. 'Any leads?'

'Not yet.'

'Well, we need something quickly.'

'Good idea, sir.'

'Don't be facetious, Jack. I'll need something for when I get there.'

Harris closed his eyes. 'I'm not sure that's entirely necess—'

'I do not care what you think. I have just finished my meeting at headquarters and not surprisingly the chief constable was eager for information. I'll be there within the hour.'

'Looking forward to it already,' said Harris and clicked the end call button on his phone. He looked at the dogs. 'That's all I need.'

Having let the animals out to wander round the car park for a few minutes, the inspector sat in the driver's seat and stared moodily at the hills. Not for the first time that day, he wished he was up there. You could trust the hills. You could also trust Leckie. He dialled a number on his mobile.

'It's Hawk,' he said.

'Not wanting me to solve another of your crimes, are you? Someone nick a sheep?'

'Not quite,' said Harris as he settled back in the seat. Same joke every time. Graham Leckie was one of the few people who could get away with such banter. 'But I do need your help.'

'Shoot.'

A uniformed constable with Greater Manchester Police, Leckie was one of the inspector's closest friends, the two men initially connecting some years previously through their love of wildlife. Even when Harris had moved north, they talked regularly on the phone because Leckie worked in force intelligence and the valley regularly witnessed crimes committed by criminals coming into the area from further south. Harris had already decided where to look for his killer.

'I want to talk medals,' said the inspector.

'Don't tell me someone has been stupid enough to award you one?'

'Got a dead war hero on my hands.'

'Ouch.' There was a change in Leckie's tone. More businesslike. 'They'll be coming out of the woodwork on that one. How can I help?'

'Someone lifted this guy's VC and I wondered if any of your lot might be in the frame for it? This job has big city stamped all over it and I really do need an early break. The media are all over this like a rash and my commander is already riding up the valley on a white horse.'

'I'll bet he is. Nothing stirs up folks like a dead war hero, especially one with a VC to his name. And we're only three days away from Remembrance Sunday, don't forget.'

'Like I could forget it. The locals have already gone into meltdown, which is why I really do need to get the lid on this PDQ. I've got old folks worrying themselves sick that the Day of Judgment is upon us.'

'Well, there's certainly one or two down here like their memorabilia. Big black market in the stuff. Let me try something.' Harris could hear Leckie tapping on his computer keyboard. 'Thought I remembered something about it. There's a bunch working out of Manchester. Did a ninety-one-year-old at the start of the year. Took his medals. Poor guy was in hospital for five weeks. Disturbed them in his bedroom in the middle of the night and had a go. Got his head banged off the edge of a table for his trouble.'

'Sounds familiar. He dead?'

'He's in a home, by the looks of it. Suffered three strokes in hospital.'

'Your lot get them?'

'Got two guys for it. They're inside awaiting trial.' Harris heard more tapping. 'The DI on the case – lad called Jamie Standish—'

'He made DI, did he? Not surprised, mind, he always was a good officer. I was the one who made him sergeant, you know.'

'Not the only thing you made, as I recall.'

'Yes, well, we don't talk about that, Graham.'

'He does.'

'Ah.'

'Anyway, moving on swiftly,' said Leckie but Harris could hear in his voice that he was smiling, 'it says here that the old guy might not be well enough to give evidence which means the case would collapse. They left precious little at the house. Bunch of pros, apparently.'

'Pros don't beat old men up, Graham. Not sure this helps me if he's got them locked up, mind.'

'Not so fast. According to this, Jamie reckons there were others involved. A nightclub doorman on his way home from work saw four people in a car near the old fellow's house on the night it happened. Challenged them and they drove off. Looks like they came back later.'

'Got any names on the two that got away?'

'The ones we nicked stayed schtum, as you would expect, but Jamie says they have a couple of associates that fit the bill. David Forrest's one. We reckon he was the driver. Name ring a bell?'

"Fraid not. What's his story?'

'Usual thing. Record as long as your arm. Robbery, assault, aggravated burglary … it goes on and on. This lad's a real piece of work.'

'What's more, he has no respect for traffic law.'

'Come again?'

'I think our lot may have stopped him in Levton Bridge yesterday with a tail light out. Not that I'm very hopeful of that producing much. I'd put money on false ID. And the other guy?'

'An old friend of yours, I think. One Ronald William Michaels. I seem to remember that you banged him up for doing lorries on the M62.'

'I certainly did,' said Harris, scowling as he glanced out of the window to see Elaine Landy interviewing a couple of villagers next to the war memorial. 'Tried to make out that he was not a violent man but still managed to cosh an HGV driver. Where are they now? Do we know?'

'Not been seen since the job. It says here that Standish reckons they left the city.'

'Well, I have this awful feeling I know where they were last night,' said Harris. 'Can you send me something over on them, Graham? Mug shots would be nice.'

'Consider it done, matey.'

'Oh, can you check one more thing?' said Harris. 'No, forget I said it. It's daft.'

'Try me. I know you're daft anyway.'

'Yeah, but I really am flying a kite here. We've got a local tea-leaf, strictly small stuff. Bloke called Lenny Portland. He's been hanging round the village where our old chap was murdered.'

'Let me check,' said Leckie and again there was a tapping sound. 'Portland. Portland. No, nothing. Sorry about that, old son.'

'Thanks for looking anyway. It was always going to be a long—'

'Let me try something else.' There was silence for a few moments then, 'Well, well, that's interesting.'

Harris sat forward in his seat. 'What is?' he asked.

'Seems like Ronny Michaels may indeed have an associate from your neck of the woods. There was an unknown face seen with him a couple of times last year and our lot followed him to the railway station where he bought a ticket for Roxham. That's further down the valley from you, isn't it?'

'It's where you change if you want to get up to Levton Bridge.'

'Thought you needed a time machine for that,' said Leckie.

'Yes, thanks for that, Graham. Did your lot get a decent look at the face?'

'Not really. It didn't fit in with any known associates so they lost interest.'

'Well, I'm interested.'

A few seconds later, Jack Harris was striding across the

green towards Gallagher and Butterfield, who were standing watching the force mobile incident room parking up alongside the green.

'Stop that bus,' said the inspector to a startled Gallagher, pointing in the direction of Levton Bridge.

'This isn't the Chuckle Brothers,' said the sergeant without thinking. And immediately regretted it.

'Will you just stop that fucking bus?' snapped the inspector.

'Which bus?' asked Gallagher, trying to sound serious.

Harris looked at Butterfield. 'The one the constable here let Lenny Portland get on,' he said. 'See, there may be more to our Mr Portland than meets the eye.'

Gallagher and Butterfield exchanged dubious glances.

'Are we talking about the same Lenny Portland?' asked Gallagher.

'For God's sake, am I the only one who has worked out that we are investigating a murder here?'

'No, of course not,' said Gallagher hurriedly, 'it's just that Lenny Portland is small fry.'

'But maybe his friends aren't. Had you ever thought of that?'

'On my way,' said Gallagher, urgent now and turning to jog to his vehicle. After a few paces, he glanced back. 'Oh, Esther Morritt wants to talk to you.'

'What about?'

'Says she will only talk to you. Says you know what you're doing.'

'Well, she'll have to wait,' said Harris. 'Just stop that bus then we can think about Esther Morritt.'

'Says she knows who killed Harold Leach.'

'And I wonder,' said the inspector, 'who she reckons did that then?'

'I imagine you think that I am some kind of madwoman,' said Esther Morritt, as she sat on the sofa in the gloomy front room of her cottage. She did not look at Harris but stared instead at the threadbare carpet.

'I wouldn't have said ...'

'Oh, come on,' said Esther, finally looking at the inspector as he sat on a scruffy armchair, grubby cup and saucer balanced on his lap. 'Everyone else thinks I'm mad. You ask your sergeant what he thinks about me. Why should you be any different?'

'You have not exactly been acting rationally, have you?' Harris took a sip of tea. 'And there's plenty of folks out there think you vandalized the memorial last night.'

'Well, I didn't.' She seemed horrified at the thought. 'There's no way I would dishonour the memory of those men. That could have been Philip's name up there.'

'But that's the point, isn't it, Esther?' He glanced at the photograph hanging on the wall. A young man in uniform. Sallow complexion, the remnants of acne, greasy hair. 'It isn't his name up there, is it? Like it or not, your son brought about his own death by drinking himself silly.'

'Have you ever lost a child, Inspector?' She looked at him intently.

Harris shook his head. 'Doesn't change the facts, though, does it?' he said.

'You sound like Rob Mackey. That's the kind of thing he'd say.'

'Nevertheless, that's what this has all been about, hasn't it?' Now it was the inspector's turn to look intently at her. 'You can't face the fact that his father died a hero and gets his name on a memorial and that your son did not. I kind of side with Rob Mackey on this one, much as it galls me to say it.'

'How can you say that?' said Esther, eyes flashing with anger. 'That man murdered my son! Why will no one listen to what I have to say?'

'Because it just does not make sense,' said Harris wearily. 'Oh, give over, Esther, don't give me the look. My sergeant examined every bit of evidence. It was a very thorough invest—'

'He saw what he wanted to see. You have to believe me when I say he missed it.'

'But missed what?' said an exasperated inspector. 'The medical evidence showed that Philip had drunk enough to knock out a bull elephant and that his injuries were consistent with a fall.'

'I am not disputing that but I think that when my son was walking past Laurel House, what really happened is that Rob Mackey came out and attacked him then left him to die and came back later and pretended to ...'

'Yes, but the medical evidence simply does not support that, Esther. And Mackey's wife swore blind that he did not leave their bed. She should know.'

'A wife does not know everything.'

'OK, I've heard enough.' Harris drained his cup and stood up. 'I have no intention of going over old ground, Esther. Next thing you'll be telling me that Rob Mackey murdered Harold.'

'That is exactly what I am telling you. And what's more, I can prove it.'

*

Matty Gallagher guided his car at speed along the narrow country road, struggling to keep the vehicle off the grass verge as it rocked and rolled. Sitting in the passenger seat, Alison Butterfield leaned forward eagerly, her eyes gleaming with the excitement of the chase.

'You're gaining on it!' she said.

'It is only a service bus,' said Gallagher, steering sharply as they approached a bend. 'It's hardly Bullitt.'

'You do have a look of Steve McQueen in the right light,' said Butterfield as the vehicle careered round a tight bend. 'I've always thought it. Mind you, he wasn't going bald.'

'Yes, thank you, Constable.' Gallagher glanced in his rear-view mirror to see it filled with a patrol car, siren blaring, headlights flashing. 'It would seem that not everyone appreciates my driving, though.'

As the patrol car overtook them, narrowly avoiding scraping along the dry-stone wall, the sergeant noted the grinning figure of Roger Barnett.

'Flash git,' said Butterfield.

'Dangerous flash git,' said Gallagher.

Rob Mackey sat on a sofa in the living room at Laurel House with his eyes closed and his head throbbing. He had been there ever since arriving home following his angry confrontation with Harris outside the cottage in Chapel Hill. Mackey had known that it was a risk to demand that Harris arrest Esther Morritt, had known that it would only serve to infuriate the inspector, but it was all he could think of to buy him the time he needed to get his thoughts straight. He knew the time had come to act. The letter had changed everything and Mackey was sure that the police would be called in sometime. Maybe they already had been; maybe they were just waiting for their moment. Maybe the death of

Harold Leach had distracted them. But he knew it would not be for long. If not today, tomorrow....

The silence of the room was disturbed by the sound of a police siren in the distance and Mackey snapped open his eyes and cursed. He knew that he should have fled the valley when the envelope arrived. He had wrestled with the idea at the time but family loyalty had kept him there, a strong feeling that he needed to see the unveiling of the memorial through, that he owed it to his father's memory to complete the task. His father. Mackey sighed; what would his father think of what he had done? To honour the dead? The son had hardly honoured the father. Or his mother's memory, for that matter. Dead from cancer within three years of her husband's death. The thought came with a stab of guilt and Mackey listened as the sirens grew louder.

He relaxed slightly as the emergency vehicle passed the house and the siren faded away into the direction of Levton Bridge. The moment did not last long, however, and he stood up. Mackey knew that Harris would come for him sooner or later. That's what Roger Barnett was trying to tell him at the ceremony. Mackey walked over to the bureau, where he opened a drawer from which he extracted a pen and writing paper. He sat down.

'Dear Liz and Bethany,' he wrote. 'I should have written this letter a long time ago. I am afraid that I have done something rather stupid....'

'What on earth has Rob Mackey got to do with the murder of Harold Leach?' asked Harris, looking dubiously at Esther but not sitting down. 'You're paranoid, woman, you really are.'

'Do you know why Harold was killed, Inspector?'

'I do not really think that it is any of your business.'

'Was it for his VC?'

'What makes you say that?'

'Well, was it?' She looked at him intently. 'For the medal?'

'Yes.' Harris nodded, finally sitting down, something in her tone piquing his interest. 'Yes, we think it probably was.'

'Then whoever took it will have to sell it somewhere, I imagine.' She raised an eyebrow. 'I believe the criminal fraternity refers to the practice as fencing, do they not?'

'They do but I am still ...'

'So you will presumably be asking yourself who around here deals in war memorabilia?'

'That would certainly be one line of inquiry but no one that I am aware of—'

'Rob Mackey does.'

'Oh, come on, Esther!' exclaimed Harris, standing up again. 'I have more important things to do than listen to you trying to rope Rob Mackey into everything that happens. For a start, as far as I know he deals in antique furniture. To the best of my knowledge, he has no interest in medals.'

'Ah, but he does,' said Esther as the detective headed for the door. 'He may not advertise the fact but he does.'

'Even if he did ...' said Harris, pausing with his hand on the door knob. Despite himself, he found himself intrigued at what she was saying. He returned to the armchair and gave her a wry look. She had him hooked and they both knew it and, in that moment, for the first time, Harris found himself experiencing the stirrings of respect for Esther Morritt. 'OK, let's assume that I agree it's interesting. Just means I'm covering my back. Everyone knows you don't like the man. You've accused him of every crime under the sun and there is no evidence of—'

'What if I had evidence?'

'You haven't produced it so far.'

'So far.'

She walked over to the dresser and produced a beige folder

from which she removed a sheet of white paper. She handed it to Harris.

'I only found it yesterday,' she said. Her voice trembled slightly. 'After the inquest. It was the first time I could bring myself to look through Philip's things. I had no idea it was there.'

Harris scanned the scrawled handwriting in silence.

'I was going to contact you about it this morning,' she continued, 'then poor Harold was found and I did not have the chance. At first I thought it just linked Mackey to the death of my son but it does cast an interesting light on Harold's murder as well. Does it not?'

'Possibly.' He tried to make the reply sound noncommittal.

'I take it you realize what it is?'

Jack Harris nodded.

'It is,' he said, looking at her with a half smile on his face, 'what the likes of me would call evidence, Esther.'

'I think it probably is, Inspector.' She did not seek to conceal the look of triumph on her face. 'I think it probably is.'

Having left Gallagher and Butterfield behind, Roger Barnett flung his car into another corner, passed the bus at speed, slammed his foot on the brake and slewed the police vehicle to a juddering halt across the road. As the startled bus driver jammed his foot on the brake, the sergeant leapt from his car and ran towards the vehicle.

'What the bloody hell do you think you are doing, Roger?' exclaimed the driver angrily as Barnett clambered up the steps of the bus. 'You could have got us all killed!'

'Lenny Portland!' said Barnett, ignoring the comment and pointing down the bus towards his quarry. 'Come here!'

Matty Gallagher brought his car to a halt behind the bus and looked aghast at the skid marks showing where the vehicle had skidded to a halt.

'Come on,' said the detective sergeant, wrenching open his door. 'God knows what Rambo will do in this mood.'

He and Butterfield ran down the side of the bus. As they did so, Gallagher glanced up and noticed the frightened face of Lenny Portland staring back at him out of the grimy window. The sight of Gallagher seemed to galvanize Portland into action and he disappeared from view. As the detectives reached the front of the bus, Barnett staggered down the stairs, cursing and clutching his bloodied nose, followed by Lenny Portland who barged past him. Portland evaded Gallagher's grasp and started to run down the road.

'Bastard,' snarled Barnett and turned to give chase only to be blocked by Matty Gallagher, whose intervention allowed Butterfield to race past both of them.

'Get out of my way,' snarled Barnett as he bundled the detective sergeant aside.

'I think you've done enough for one day,' said Gallagher angrily.

Barnett brushed past him and Gallagher turned to watch him struggling to catch up with the fleet-footed young constable as she closed in on Portland before launching a rugby tackle which sent him crashing to the ground. Gallagher winced as he heard Portland's head crack against the tarmac. Ignoring Portland's pained protests, Butterfield subdued the struggling thief and cuffed his arms behind his back. She turned to survey the approaching Barnett, who had blood dripping from his battered nose and staining his tunic.

'Sometimes,' she said, grinning, 'a bit of youth comes in really handy in these situations. What do you reckon, Roger?'

Barnett said nothing but dabbed his nose. Matty Gallagher smiled as he walked up to join them. He did not care that Roger Barnett saw the gesture.

*

'I take it you know *exactly* what it is?' asked Esther Morritt as Harris continued to study the sheet of paper.

'It appears to be some form of ledger. Items sold.'

'Why so coy, Inspector? Surely you can see that some of them are medals?'

'OK, Esther, yes, medals. Three of them, it would seem.'

'And look at the last date, Inspector. Three days before my son died. It grieves me to say it because I doted on the boy but I think Philip was in league with Rob Mackey. I think that Philip might have been handling medals for him.' Esther hesitated. 'Maybe even stolen ones.'

'Perhaps stealing them himself,' said Harris, looking at her. 'Is that possible, do you think, Esther? Was your son stealing medals?'

'It's a big leap of logic, Inspector.'

'It's all a big leap of logic.' Harris tapped the piece of paper. 'For a start, this does not mention Rob Mackey's name. It doesn't mention your son, for that matter. This could have been written by anyone. It could even have been faked. Perhaps by someone with a reason to blacken the name of Rob Mackey.'

'Why would I do that? And if I was going to fake something to implicate Rob Mackey, do you not think that I would have put his name on it somewhere?'

'Maybe but ...'

'One thing is for certain, it's Philip's handwriting. See how he gets the "a" the wrong way round? He always did that. Right from when he was in primary school. Used to drive his teachers crazy. I can supply other examples of his writing.'

'Even if ...'

'Do you want to know what I think?' She did not wait to hear the answer. Her words came quickly now and brooked no interruption. Nor did the inspector try to halt the flow. 'I think Philip grew sick of selling those things, what with being in the army and everything. He was a good boy and I think he knew that he had done wrong. I think he was ashamed and tried to get out. I think Philip told Mackey and Mackey killed him to stop him saying anything.'

She paused, her energies temporarily spent. Harris seized his opportunity.

'Now who's doing the big leap of logic, Esther?' he said. 'I cannot see how it links Mackey to the murder of Harold Leach.'

'Ah, but what if Mackey thought he had got away with it? He may well have thought that when he saw the way you all dismissed my comments out of hand. Might not a VC have tempted him?'

'You seem to have thought this through very thoroughly, Esther.'

'You do a lot of thinking when you are on your own, Inspector.'

Matty Gallagher stood on the edge of the road and watched the departure of Roger Barnett's vehicle, bound for Levton Bridge with Butterfield and Lenny Portland in the back. As it disappeared round the bend, Gallagher heard a guttural sound behind him and turned to see the service bus rumble forward, belching black smoke out of its exhaust. The detective sergeant waved at the driver, who did not reciprocate, then returned to his own vehicle. As he lowered himself into the passenger seat, a Range Rover drove past, hardly slowing as it squeezed through the narrow gap between the detective's car and the stone wall, clipping his wing mirror as it did so.

'Hey!' shouted the sergeant, getting out again to remonstrate and noticing that the driver was a grim-faced Rob Mackey.

Deep in thought, Gallagher stood in the middle of the road again, watching as the Range Rover disappeared round the bend. What had that expression been on Mackey's face? he asked himself. Uneasiness? Anxiety? No, thought the sergeant, no, it was stronger than that. The look on Rob Mackey's face had been one of fear. Gallagher toyed with going after him but decided against it. After all, he decided, as he got back into his car, what would he say?

CHAPTER TEN

It was a troubled Jack Harris who emerged from Esther Morritt's cottage and started to walk down the street as the gloom began to descend on the village. The inspector's disquiet had been triggered because, although he did not generally believe in certainties – he had seen too much for such fanciful notions – he had nevertheless always believed that on the night of his death, Philip Morritt drank too much and hit his head. Harris had heard Esther's protestations and her wild accusations – he could not avoid them even if he wanted to, no one in the valley could – but at no point had he doubted that Matty Gallagher had got it right. It had been, in the inspector's opinion, a well-run investigation; Harris would have expected nothing less from an officer whose abilities he had grown to respect in the two years since the sergeant had arrived in the valley.

Besides, thought Harris, nodding at the uniformed officer standing at the front door to Harold Leach's cottage as he walked into the hallway, the coroner had agreed that Gallagher had come to the right conclusion. Even the notoriously hard-to-please Curtis had concurred. Open and shut case, everyone said, and Harris had seen no reason to disagree. But now this, thought Harris, as he walked into the front room and gloomily surveyed the overturned furniture, now this....

'Sir,' said a voice and the inspector turned as one of the forensics officers walked into the room behind him.

'Anything?' asked Harris hopefully. 'Believe me, anything will do.'

'Something that does not quite make sense, I am afraid.'

'I don't need any more mysteries. Curtis will be here in a few minutes and he'll have a haemorrhage if I don't have anything.'

'Sorry.'

'What's the mystery then?'

'Your mate in GMP reckons there might be two of them, right?'

'We haven't got anything definite to link Forrest and Michaels to this job as yet, but yes. It's certainly their MO. Why?'

'We think there may have been three. See, we bagged a lot of fibres but when we cross-checked with the old man's clothes, that leaves us with three garments unaccounted for. Jumpers, most like. Sorry, but you've got someone else in here.'

'Where'd you find them?'

'All in the bedroom. Two close to the body, the third snagged on the edge of the old feller's chest of drawers. We'll see what the lab comes up with.'

'You finished then?' said Harris, glancing at the metal case in his hand.

'Not much more we can do here.'

'Thanks for your efforts, Charlie.'

'Make sure you get him,' said the forensics man. 'The old feller didn't deserve this. Not after what he did.'

Harris nodded and listened to the officers departing the cottage. When they had gone, silence settled on the darkening little room and the detective stood in silence, letting the atmosphere of the cottage wash over him as he appreciated being alone for the first time since his walk across the moor that morning. Harris liked being alone, always had, helped him think, and he glanced around at the disturbed furniture, trying to get a clear picture of the intruders at work. Trying to put Ronny Michaels in the place. Was this his style? Harris recalled visiting the coshed lorry driver in hospital after the M62 job and gave a slight nod. He recalled Leckie's account of the old man done over in Manchester and all for a medal. Yes, thought Harris, he could see Ronny Michaels in this place. As the silence lengthened, the inspector closed his eyes but all he could see was the face of Harold Leach.

'We'll get him, my old friend,' murmured Harris. 'I promise.'

'I imagine you will,' said a woman's voice.

The inspector started and turned to see Harold Leach's granddaughter standing in the doorway. Her eyes were red from crying.

'Maggie,' he said. 'You startled me.'

'Sorry.'

'They told me you were working out of the area.'

'I was running a seminar in Birmingham. A couple of traffic officers brought me up.' Maggie looked at the scene of devastation and shook her head. 'What a mess. He was such a tidy man, Inspector. He would have hated this.'

She reached into her handbag for a handkerchief with which she dabbed her eyes.

'He did not deserve to die like this,' she added. 'Really, he didn't.'

'No, he didn't, love.'

'He was such a sweet old man,' she said, sitting on the sofa. 'Never harmed anyone.'

'Except in war.' For a moment, Harris wondered if she would object to the comment but she did not appear to.

'Let's just say he told me that he never harmed anyone then,' she said with a slight smile. 'Six years in the army and he did not kill anyone. Can you believe that?'

'I can.'

'You were in the army. Did you ever kill anyone?'

'I think you will find that it is something soldiers do not talk about.'

'I guess I just have to take my grandfather's word for it then.' She looked at the photographs on the wall. 'Too late to ask him now.'

There was an awkward silence, broken by Harris.

'I am really sorry about what has happened here, I really am,' he said.

'I heard you promise him,' she said with a slight smile. 'My grandfather would have appreciated that, Inspector.'

'Least I can do.'

'Your sergeant, Gallagher I think his name was, he said on the phone that I might have to identify my grandfather's body? Is he here?'

'We thought it best to remove him as quickly as we could. You know what people are like round here.'

'There's still a few hanging around outside.' She nodded. 'And that TV reporter tried to collar me again. She was most insistent but I told her to leave me alone. So where is he? Where is my grandfather?'

'The General at Roxham. We'll have to take you down there. Sorry about this, it's never a pleasant thing to have to do.'

'No need to apologize, Inspector. I had to do the same for my grandmother. Fifty-nine years they'd been married, can you believe that? Got married just after the war. She was a nurse. They met somewhere in North Africa. He did tell me the name of the place but I forget it now.'

'Sidi Omar.'

'That's it.' She smiled at him. 'Harold had a lot of time for you, Jack. He said you were one of the good guys.'

'Right.' Harris stood in silence for a few moments; he never knew what to say in such situations. He walked over to stare at the picture of Harold wearing his VC. 'I am really sorry, Maggie, but I do have to ask some questions before we take you down to Roxham.'

'I understand. What do you want to know?'

'Had Harold had trouble?'

'Trouble?' She looked surprised. 'What kind of trouble?'

'You know, anyone trying to take things from him?'

'Things?'

'His medals. His VC.'

'Is that what this is about?' she asked.

'We think so.'

'That thing!' she exclaimed, surprising the inspector with her vehemence. 'I told him not to keep it in the house. I said he should keep it in a safe deposit box down the bank but he would not have any of it. Couldn't believe that anyone would take it from him. Said people respected what it meant too much for that.'

'You didn't agree, clearly. Why?'

'I knew it was valuable. There'd been offers.'

Harris walked over to sit next to her on the sofa. 'Offers?' he said.

'Yes, a couple of years ago. Two in six months. Memorabilia dealers, offering to buy it. They said a VC would fetch a good price. He had another one a few weeks ago as well, after that blessed documentary came out.'

'You did not approve of it?'

'No, I didn't. I told him, I said that it could only draw attention to him but he just could not see it. They're so naïve, old folks, aren't they?'

'They can be, yes. These approaches, do you have any names?'

She shook her head. 'Sorry,' she said.

'Clearly, he refused to sell.'

'Of course he did. Wouldn't have been parted from the thing for all the tea in China.' She smiled. 'That was his favourite phrase.'

'Did they come back, any of these guys? Particularly the most recent one?'

'Not as far as I know. And no, before you ask, I do not have their descriptions. My grandfather's sight was pretty poor.' She gave the inspector a sad look. 'We suggested that he should go into a home but he refused.'

'Were there any other incidents? Break-ins? There's nothing in our records to suggest there was.'

'The odd scallywag round the door over the years. Remember that bloke pretending to be from the gas board?'

'When was that?'

'Maybe it was before you came back. My grandfather hit him with his walking stick. Broke the bloke's nose. There was a piece in the paper about it.' She chuckled. '"Handy Harold" the headline called him. Once a fighter, always a fighter, I guess.'

Harris thought of the body lying in the mortuary.

'So it would seem,' he said.

Ten minutes later, he strode towards his Land Rover where he opened the rear of the vehicle to release the dogs, watching them as they headed off onto the green, sniffing their way across the damp grass. The inspector turned as he heard a car drive into the village, its headlights cutting through the gathering gloom and illuminating the swirling flecks of rain. Harris smiled a welcome as Gallagher got out and walked over to the inspector.

'Uniform are taking Maggie down to Roxham,' said Harris. 'How did you find her?'

'Wonders of the internet. She runs her own training company and was doing a seminar for a load of shop-girls.'

'Good work,' said Harris, walking round to the back of the Land Rover and bringing out two bowls and a tin of dog food.

'No, really, I've already eaten,' said Gallagher. 'Had a sandwich from the bakery in Levton Bridge. Mind, I suspect a bowl of Pedigree Chum would be tastier than their cheese and ham.'

'Funny man,' said Harris and together they headed for the mobile incident room parked nearby.

Seeing them go, the dogs ran over to the vehicle, Scoot leading the way with Archie struggling and scrabbling his way up the steps.

'Daft bugger,' said Harris, noticing the dog's difficulties and affectionately dragging him up by his collar as he threatened to slip back, tongue sticking out with his exertions.

'Not the most athletic specimen, is he?' said Gallagher, watching Harris fill the bowls and place them on the floor. 'Mind, not sure that Curtis will like the idea of them being ...'

The sergeant held up his hands as he saw the inspector's expression.

'OK, I know,' said Gallagher. 'I know, your problem.'

'I like to think,' said Harris, sitting down at one of the tables, 'that our beloved commander is everybody's problem. It's one of my driving motivations in life. So, you got Lenny Portland then?'

'Roger Barnett did his Jack Regan stuff. There's a huge skid mark on the road,' said the sergeant, walking over to the sink. 'That guy really is a tosser, you know. Could have really hurt someone with his antics this afternoon. There was no need for it. It was only a clapped-out service bus, for God's sake.'

'He's a loose cannon, Matty lad.' Harris ruffled Scoot's head as the dog wandered over, having wolfed down his tea. 'Likes the uniform too much, if you ask me. Thinks he's a law to his own.'

Gallagher paused. Having seen the way Harris went about his policing, what the sergeant really wanted to say was 'kettle or pot?' but he decided against it. Instead, with the kettle in question in his hand, he turned to face the inspector.

'Tea?' he said.

'Aye, go on. So where's Portland now?'

'Butterfield took him through to Levton Bridge.'

'He say anything?'

'Not unless you count questioning Barnett's parentage.'

'I thought he'd be more hacked off that Butterfield damn near fractured his skull.'

'Oddly enough, no. He seems to have a soft spot for Alison. I reckon he fancies her.' He grinned. 'Hey, perhaps he's her fancy man?'

'Somehow I think not.'

'You want her to interview him anyway?'

'No, I'll do it later. We've got something else to think about first.' Harris hesitated. 'I am not sure that you are going to like what I am about to say, Matty lad.'

'Oh?' Gallagher turned round, box of teabags in hand. 'What's that then?'

'I've just been with Esther,' said Harris, lowering his voice even though they were alone in the vehicle. 'She reckons that Mackey could be behind the murder of Harold Leach.'

'Oh, come on!'

'Might not be as daft as it sounds.'

'Surely you didn't actually listen to any of her claptrap?' exclaimed Gallagher, aghast. 'I thought we had established that the woman is off her rocker? You'll be telling me that she shot President Kennedy next! She the old woman on the grassy knoll then?'

'Hear me out,' said Harris calmly, taking the piece of paper out of his coat pocket and placing it on the table. It was in a plastic bag now. 'Belonged to Philip Morritt, apparently. It's only just turned up.'

'How convenient.' Gallagher leaned over to examine the document for a few moments. 'OK, it appears to relate to the sale of items including medals but not sure that it proves Mackey was involved. Unless I am missing something.'

'Esther says you did. Claims Mackey and her son were in cahoots and that Mackey killed him to keep him quiet. Now, if—'

'If,' interrupted Gallagher. He sounded defensive now. 'If.'

'It's a big if, granted, but if she is right, that could put him in the frame for Harold's murder.'

'Conspiracy theories, guv.'

'Imagine you were running this investigation and another officer brought this to you. What would you say to them?'

Gallagher said nothing as he finished making the tea and brought the mugs over.

'Do I take it,' he said, sitting down next to the inspector, 'that you are going to re-open the Morritt inquiry?'

'What option do I have?'

'That means you do not believe that I did a good job,' said Gallagher quietly. 'I mean, that's what folks will say, won't they? That Esther Morritt was right all along and that the wide-boy southerner wouldn't listen to her. I'll be a laughing stock.'

'When did we ever take any notice of what people say about us? Besides, we just say new evidence has emerged.'

'Perhaps we should have searched the kid's belongings after he died. We just assumed it was an accident.'

'Why think anything else?' said Harris, taking a sip of tea.

'But if it ends up being genuine and ... Hey, Mackey passed me after Rambo stopped the bus. If Esther's right, he wasn't popping down the supermarket for a loaf of bread.'

'Best get back out there,' said Harris, standing up as Gallagher headed for the door just as Philip Curtis emerged at the top of the steps.

'What's the emergency?' asked the commander, scowling as he noticed the dogs.

'Possible breakthrough,' said Harris.

'Which is?'

'We think Rob Mackey may be involved in the murder.'

'You think what?' Curtis stared at the inspector in amazement. He looked at Gallagher. 'You agree?'

Gallagher hesitated.

'I'll take that as a no,' said the superintendent, turning back to Harris. 'Everyone knows you've got it in for Mackey but the man has proved himself remarkably generous to this community and we should not harass him because of some silly vendetta....'

Gallagher made his mind up.

'Actually,' said the sergeant, 'I think the DCI may have a point. We certainly can't take the chance, can we?'

Harris shot his colleague a grateful look.

'Yes, well, it sounds pretty far-fetched to me,' said Curtis grudgingly. 'I mean why would you think this?'

'Esther Morritt says ...' began the inspector.

'Is she really the best you can do?'

'We have also arrested Lenny Portland.'

'The man's a petty thief. I'd hardly call it progress, would you?'

Harris did not reply but watched balefully as Curtis walked over to stare out of the vehicle window. The commander's gaze settled on the small knot of people gathered round the defaced war memorial, now being filmed by the camera crew.

'And the vandalism?' said Curtis, turning back to the detectives. 'That linked to the murder, do you think?'

'It's still early days,' said Harris but he knew that it sounded lame.

In the ensuing silence, the inspector found himself searching for something with which to fight back, something with which to impress the commander. The sensation surprised the inspector, whose usual approach was to divulge as little as possible to Curtis in an attempt to reduce the amount of what he saw as his meddling in investigations. 'This inquiry will run on a need-to-know basis,' the inspector would always tell his staff, tapping the side of his nose, 'and that sanctimonious bastard does not need to know anything.' But this was different. Harris knew that an entire community was looking to him to come up with something. Knew that his commander would be feeling the same. Knew that what Curtis really wanted was something to ease his own fears. And wanted it quickly. Everyone did. Yet again, Harris recalled the seminar.

'There is another line of inquiry,' said Harris. 'But there's nothing to confirm it at this stage. There is the possibility that whoever killed Harold came from outside the area. That they were after his VC.'

'Outside? Where outside?'

'Manchester.'

'That sounds more likely,' said Curtis. There was something different about him now, less confrontational, more understanding. Hopeful. 'That makes a lot more sense.'

Harris nodded; it seemed the most politically sensible thing to do.

'We really do have to sort this out quickly,' continued Curtis earnestly. 'People are panicking. Control have already taken calls from pensioners saying they are frightened to stay at home. And it's not just Chapel Hill either. We have had them from other villages. And the media are lapping it up. You know what something like this does.'

'I've asked uniform to make a big show of patrolling here tonight and to keep an eye on the other war memorials in the area. Last thing we want is another incident.'

'Let's hope we don't get one then,' said Curtis, walking back down the steps. 'In the meantime, I suggest you get this sorted quickly. And don't waste any more time on this Mackey thing. Results, Jack, we need results.'

'Yes, sir,' said Harris glumly.

'So,' said Gallagher when the commander had gone, 'I take it that means you do not want to reopen the inquiry into Philip Morritt's death after all?'

'Not for the moment, but I do want Mackey brought in, mind. Whichever way this breaks, he still has some questions to answer. Put the word out, will you?'

'But Curtis said ...'

'I know what he said,' said Harris, noticing the sergeant's uncertainty. 'Do it for me, will you? Go and see the wife, yeah? Get Butterfield to meet you there. A woman's touch and all that.'

Gallagher nodded. 'Sure,' he said, and headed out of the incident room.

When he had gone and silence had settled on the vehicle, Jack Harris walked over to his dogs.

'Poor old Harold,' he said, kneeling down and ruffling their heads. 'He did not deserve this. No one deserves this.'

The inspector felt tears start in his eyes. He had been fighting them all day. Harold Leach was not simply a number, not just another victim of crime to be processed. Harold Leach had been a friend. A good friend and one to be mourned. Wiping his eyes with the back of his hand, Harris straightened up and walked towards the door. The dogs followed him out onto the green where the inspector stood for a few moments in the rain and let his gaze roam to the looming shapes of the hills gradually disappearing as darkness settled on the North Pennines. Even though they were fading from view, Harris could visualize them perfectly, see every path, every copse, every dry-stone wall, every brook. The inspector had walked them so many times that he had lost count and now, as he stood on the grass, he felt their pull once more, felt them drawing him in, urging him to forget the stresses of the real world and give himself up to their embrace. Sometimes, thought Harris, as he allowed himself to experience the moment, it would be all too easy to give in to their gentle caresses. Hand in his badge, retire, find something else to do, something different, something where he did not have to deal with man's inhumanity to man. He sighed.

'Sir?'

The woman's voice broke into his reverie and Harris turned slowly and surveyed the young uniformed constable standing at a respectful distance.

'Are you all right, sir?'

'Why should I not be?'

'You seemed not to have heard me. It was the third time I'd tried to speak to you.'

'Do you go walking, Constable?'

She seemed taken aback by the question. 'Walking, sir?'

He gestured to the dark shapes disappearing in the gathering gloom. 'On the hills.'

'Sometimes.'

'Sometimes I wish I did not have to come back.'

She looked at him uncertainly. 'Are you sure you are all right, sir?'

Harris gave a slight smile. 'Yes, of course I am. What did you want me for?'

The inspector noticed a man in a delivery uniform standing a few feet away.

'This is Gary Ross, sir,' said the constable. She gestured to the nearby streets. 'He lives in one of the cottages. He's only just got back home. Says he was out and about early this morning when he saw someone near the green.'

'Really? And why were you up so early, Mr Ross?'

'A delivery. Got quite a few early starts coming up.'

'So what time did you go out?'

'Fourish, just after. That's when I saw someone moving over there.' Ross gestured to the far side of the green. 'Fair gave me the willies, I can tell you.'

'I'm sure it did. You get a description?'

'Sorry, just saw a figure.'

'Young, old?' asked the inspector. 'Tall, short? Man, woman? Vegetable, mineral?'

'Just a figure really. It was dark; it looked kind of fuzzy.'

'Ah, one of those,' said Harris. 'Did you not think it was strange seeing someone in the village at that time of night?'

'I thought about ringing you lot but I was already late. Old Robertshaw, he don't like me to get down there late. He's a real stickler for timekeeping is old Robertshaw.'

'I'm sure he is.' The inspector looked at the young constable. 'Take a statement, will you? Oh, and when you've done that, can you get an APB out on a figure? Tell them to look for a fuzzy one.'

The constable looked at him in bemusement.

'Sir?' she said.

'It's a joke,' said Harris, turning away from her. 'I find they help to lighten the atmosphere.'

Watched by the bemused constable and followed by his dogs, Harris walked across the green. Once he was out of the constable's earshot, he murmured, 'No bloody sense of humour these young bobbies.'

Glancing down at the dogs, Harris could have sworn that Archie laughed.

CHAPTER ELEVEN

Matty Gallagher stood at the kitchen window of Laurel House and read the handwritten note for the second time. He handed it to Butterfield, who was sitting at the table. She made no comment.

'For someone unburdening himself, he doesn't say much, does he?' said Gallagher, glancing at the slight, brunette woman who was making the tea. 'What do you make of it, Mrs Mackey?'

'I have no idea,' said Liz, placing the mugs on the table.

She sounded calm, had done so ever since she had let the officers into the house. For a woman struggling with the disappearance of her husband, thought the sergeant, Liz Mackey seemed remarkably unaffected. People, he thought, reaching for his mug, you just never could work them out. Butterfield handed the note back to the sergeant but still offered no opinion on its contents. She had hardly spoken since they had arrived at the house.

'Thank you for the tea,' said Gallagher, taking a sip. 'You sure you have no idea at all why your husband would take off?'

'No.' Liz sat down at the table and looked at them. 'And he's not answering his mobile.'

For the first time, Gallagher noticed that she had been crying.

'Take all the time you need,' said the sergeant, softening his tone a little. 'I know this has been a shock.'

'I'm glad it's you,' she said quietly. Vulnerability replaced calmness.

'I'm sorry?'

'Not Jack Harris. Everyone knows that he's got it in for Rob.' She gave him a slight smile. 'I suspect you are slightly more sympathetic than your boss?'

'Only in everything,' said Gallagher. He looked back down at the note. 'This says that your husband has done something stupid and needs to get away for a while to get his thoughts straight. Had he given any indication as to what that might be?'

Liz shook her head. More tears did not seem far away.

'I know this is difficult for you,' said the sergeant, softening his tone even more. Gallagher glanced at Butterfield. 'We understand, don't we?'

'Er, yes. Yes, of course we do.'

'There you go with the sympathy,' said Liz, shooting Gallagher a grateful look.

'Sympathetic or not, I still have to ask you some questions. Had you been having ...' The sergeant hesitated. 'You know, any marital difficulties?'

'That's a very personal question.'

'Or perhaps it's something to do with your husband's business?' continued the detective. 'Was there anything to do with that? Money troubles, maybe?'

'He never talked to me about his business.'

'But surely you must know something about ...'

'I told you, I don't.' Now her tone was clipped, her vulnerability disappearing once more behind its veneer.

'Well, there must be something, Mrs Mackey,' said Gallagher, bridling slightly at her change in demeanour. 'I mean, for a husband to take off like that, there has to be something and often it's the wife who—'

'Don't you think I would have told you if I knew anything?'

'Would you have called us if we had not come round?'

'What?'

'Would you have called us?' repeated the sergeant. 'Your husband is missing, after all. Look, sometimes wives cover things up for their husbands without realizing that they would be better advised to ...'

'Don't be patronizing, Sergeant.' Liz took a sip of tea and fell silent for a few moments. 'I'm sorry. Uncalled for. I'm upset. Not thinking straight.'

'I get the impression that there *is* something you want to tell us,' said the sergeant. 'I think you know exactly what that letter is about.'

Liz began to cry again. The officers waited until she had composed herself.

'Well?' said Gallagher gently. 'What do you think has caused this?'

'I believe that he's been having an affair.'

Gallagher glanced at Butterfield, who looked out of the window.

'With who?' asked the sergeant.

'I don't know but I'm sure he is having one. A woman just knows these things.' She paused. 'Are you married, Sergeant?'

Gallagher nodded. 'Yeah,' he said, 'she's a nurse down at Roxham General.'

'And are you an attentive husband?'

'What?' Gallagher was not quite sure where the conversation was going.

'Are you an attentive husband? When was the last time you gave your wife flowers?'

'Er ... three weeks ago, I think. Not quite sure what that ...'

'Rob has never been an attentive man, Sergeant. He would not have known where to buy flowers even if he wanted to. But things have changed. I have had three bunches in the last month.' She nodded at the blooms standing in a vase on the windowsill. 'Lovely, aren't they? He even got my favourite colour right.'

'Perhaps he just realized that he had not been as—'

'You've met my husband, I take it?'

'Yes, I have.'

'Then you will have worked out that he is not the kind of man to do things like giving bunches of flowers.'

'I guess.'

'Sometimes, I wonder why I ever married him in the first place,' said Liz with a shake of the head. 'And he's got worse down the years. I mean, he's always been an arrogant man. Like father, like son. Oh, don't look like that, Constable Butterfield. Just because George won that blessed medal it does not mean that he was a good person. He was a bastard and as the years wore on, I have seen more and more of him in Rob.'

'I'm sure he's not all bad,' murmured Butterfield.

'Don't try to defend him.' Liz gave a dry laugh. 'Don't try to defend either of them. I'm glad Rob has gone. Whoever she is, she's welcome to him.'

Ten minutes later, the officers walked out of the house. Before they got into their cars, Gallagher looked at Butterfield.

'You were quiet in there,' he said.

'Sorry. Not very good in those kind of situations.'

'So much for the woman's touch.'

'Eh?'

'Nothing. What did you make of what she said?'

Butterfield shrugged. 'Maybe the governor's wrong. Maybe he's got nothing to do with what happened to Harold Leach. Maybe it's a domestic, nothing more.'

'Maybe. Listen, I'm going to nip back to Chapel Hill, see what's what. See you back at the factory.'

'Yeah, sure.'

The sergeant got into his car but before he turned the

ignition, he took his mobile phone from his jacket pocket and called up 'Jules' on his contacts. He hesitated then dialled the number.

'Hiya, love,' said a cheery voice. 'You OK?'

'Yeah, fine. You left for work yet?'

'Next few minutes. Just fed the cats and now I'm having a cup of coffee. There's some casserole in the fridge for you when you get in.'

'Thanks.' There was silence as he watched Butterfield guide her vehicle down the drive and out of sight.

'You OK?' asked Jules.

'Yeah. Yeah. Just wanted to hear your voice.'

'Oh dear, what's brought this on?'

'You know how it is sometimes,' he said.

'I do. Love you, Matty.'

'Love you, too,' said Gallagher. 'Have a good shift. See you whenever.'

'Sure. Be careful.'

The sergeant slipped the phone back in his pocket. Glancing over at the house, Gallagher saw Liz Mackey standing in the front window and staring at him. She was crying.

As Rob Mackey drove his Range Rover south across the rain-swept moorland, he slowed down to make a call on his hands-free. A woman's voice answered.

'It's me,' he said. 'Can you talk?'

'Where the hell have you been?' She sounded angry. 'The DCI has got everyone out looking for you.'

'Why?'

'He wants to talk to you about the murder of Harold Leach.'

'But I had nothing to do with that.'

'He seems to have got it into his head that you're mixed up in it somehow.'

'That man! He would believe anything about me even if ...'

'I'm sure it's all a horrible mistake, love. Why don't you just come into the station and clear it all up?'

'I can't.'

There was silence for a few moments.

'She knows about us,' said the woman.

'What?'

'Liz knows you have been having an affair. She told us.'

'Shit. She know it's you?'

'I don't think so but you know this place, it's only a matter of time. This has gone too far. You have to come in.'

There was silence on the other end of the phone.

'Rob? Rob, you there?'

'Yes, I'm here. I'm sorry, I can't come in.'

'Why not?' There was panic in her voice now. 'What have you done, for God's sake? Please God don't tell me you were involved in the murder.'

'It's more complicated than that,' said Mackey, further slowing down the Range Rover as the road dipped and twisted and he negotiated a stone bridge over a fast-flowing beck. 'I can't come in. Not yet, anyway. Got things to sort.'

'If you're tied up with the murder somehow, God help me I'll—'

'I'm not, love.' He tried to sound reassuring. 'I've told you.'

'But if you are, that puts me in a difficult situation.' She made her mind up. 'I'm sorry but I will have to tell Harris about us. I have no option.'

'No.' The voice was urgent. 'Please, don't say anything. We agreed.'

'We didn't agree anything like this.'

Mackey pulled the Land Rover onto the side of the road and cut the engine.

'Please don't,' he said quietly, the tears starting to stream down his cheeks. 'Please don't tell Harris.'

He could hear that she was crying as well. 'I have to,' she said through the tears. 'You know that.'

'But ...'

'I have to go,' said Alison Butterfield and the phone went dead.

Rob Mackey sat for a few minutes then, noticing through the gathering gloom a set of headlights behind him. He cursed, turned the key to start the engine and guided the Range Rover across the moor. Back in Levton Bridge, Butterfield sat in the deserted CID office, mobile phone still in hand, and stared wordlessly out of the window into the darkness of the night. Tears still coursed down her cheeks and she fumbled in her handbag for a handkerchief with which she dabbed her eyes.

'Damned fool,' she said quietly. 'The damned fool.'

Her reverie was disturbed by the ringing of her mobile again. She glanced down and saw the name Gallagher flash up on the screen. After letting it ring while she composed herself, she hit the receive button.

'Butterfield,' she said; her voice still sounded shaky.

'You OK?'

'Yeah, why shouldn't I be?' Butterfield hoped the reply sounded natural.

'You just sounded different.'

'Sorry about that. What you after?'

'Harris reckons there's not much more we can do out here so we're coming back in. Alan's still here anyway and he's going to stay with the incident room for a while, maybe do some more door to doors. The governor will want to talk to Lenny Portland the moment he gets back. Thought you'd like to make sure that he looks presentable.'

'Thanks,' said Butterfield, 'I will.'

'Good girl,' said Gallagher and the phone went dead.

CHAPTER TWELVE

The rain was easing as Jack Harris parked his Land Rover in front of the police station and got out of the vehicle to hear angry shouting from the direction of the market place. Running up the hill, followed by his excited dogs, the inspector was faced with the sight of a furious Henry Maitlin confronting Barry Gough and two spotty teenagers in parkas, both of whom were wielding placards as they stood in front of the town's war memorial. Gough was shouting slogans and ignoring the attempts of Maitlin to quieten him down. As Harris arrived, Maitlin made a grab for Gough's placard, sending both men staggering to the floor where they struggled on the wet cobbles.

'What the hell is going on?' shouted Harris, pushing back the dogs and wading in to separate the two men. Dragging the combatants to their feet, he let Maitlin go and surveyed his dishevelled hair. 'Brawling in the street, Henry? And at your age? Jesus H. Christ.'

Maitlin dusted the mud from his trousers and looked sheepishly at the detective.

'Sorry, Jack,' he mumbled.

Still held in the inspector's grip, and attempting to free his arm, Barry Gough showed no such contrition.

'Let go of me!' he said. 'I have my rights.'

'Not until I get some kind of answer, you haven't,' said Harris, tightening his grip.

'Ow!' squealed Gough. 'You're hurting me!'

'Then perhaps you had better give me a good explanation for your behaviour.' Harris looked at Maitlin. 'You're like a couple of four-year-olds.'

Maitlin averted his gaze and Gough finally fell silent and stopped struggling. Harris let him go.

'Well, gentlemen,' said the inspector, 'I'm waiting.'

'It's his lot,' said Maitlin, nodding at the protestors. 'Doing that in front of the war memorial like that. It's disrespectful, that's what it is, especially given what's happened to poor Harold last night.'

'We have every right to—' began Gough but cried out in pain as the inspector snapped out a hand and twisted his ear.

'Rights,' hissed the detective, 'are earned around here.'

Harris let him go again and the protestor stood a few yards away, clutching his ear. Gough's supporters edged back a pace or two when the inspector turned his attention on them. Harris estimated that neither were much above sixteen. Neither looked particularly healthy specimens. They eyed him nervously.

'And why,' said Harris, turning to Gough, 'did you decide to protest here tonight of all nights?'

'They said they were going to disrupt Sunday,' added Maitlin before any of the protestors could reply. 'Stage a demonstration in the middle of the Remembrance ceremony. It's disgraceful, Jack, absolutely disgraceful.'

'Is this true?' asked the inspector, looking at Gough again.

'Yeah, we're going to make sure that people know about the evils of—'

'Oh, do shut it,' sighed Harris. 'I really have had enough of you and your primary-school friends bleating on.'

Gough was about to remonstrate but the throbbing in his ear persuaded him to reconsider and he said nothing. The inspector turned to see Matty Gallagher walking across the market place.

'You OK, guv?' asked the sergeant, trying not to appear amused at the sight of the dishevelled Henry Maitlin trying to tidy up his hair. 'Need a hand with these hardened miscreants?'

'Think I can dispense some summary justice all on my own.'

'Right-o,' said Gallagher, turning so they could not see him smiling. He walked back across the market place, attempting to keep the laughter out of his voice. 'See you later then.'

'Now,' said Harris, returning his attention to the two men, 'I have two choices. Charge you both with fighting in the street or you can apologize for your actions. Not sure either of you fancies being charged. It would, I think, be your first conviction, Henry? Not perhaps the best advert for our local coroner, might I suggest.'

Maitlin nodded meekly. 'It won't happen again, Jack,' he said, adding with fire in his eyes, 'but I won't apologize to the likes of him.'

'And you needn't think I am either,' said Gough.

'Yeah, maybe that is asking a bit much,' said Harris, walking towards Gough until he was within six inches of him. He lowered his voice. 'If I see you anywhere near this place on Sunday your feet won't touch the ground. You can have free speech elsewhere but not in my town. You just remember that, sunshine. Now sod off.'

Gough looked as if he was about to say something but the expression on the inspector's face counselled against it and he and his fellow protestors took their placards and slunk away.

'Police state!' shouted Gough when they reached the edge of the market place.

'I like to think so,' replied Harris.

'Thank you,' said Maitlin as the protestors disappeared. It sounded heartfelt. 'I don't know what came over me, Jack.'

'You needn't think you're getting off lightly. I mean, what on earth were you thinking about? What if the press gets hold of the story?'

'I know, I know.' He looked after the retreating protestors. 'You don't think he'll tell them, do you?'

'Not if he knows what's good for him. But next time you just leave Barry Gough and his mates to me, yes?'

'You can understand why I did it, can't you, Jack?' said Maitlin, despair in his voice. 'I mean, these young people, they don't seem to understand what sacrifices we made for them. So many sacrifices, Jack, so many friends lost, and for what? So that someone like them can ...'

His voice tailed off and he closed his eyes.

'So many sacrifices,' he said quietly.

'That may be so, Henry, but there is a certain irony, is there not, that those sacrifices secured Gough and his like the right to say what they do?'

'I suppose so,' said Maitlin unhappily as they started walking towards his car, which was parked on the far side of the market place. 'But for them to do it on the day that Harold's body was discovered, it's abominable, Jack. There's no other word for it.'

He stopped walking and gave Harris a forlorn look.

'I just don't understand,' he said. 'Maybe I am too old?'

'Go home, Henry,' said the inspector gently, placing a hand on his shoulder. 'Mrs Maitlin will be wondering where you've got to. Not sure brawling on the street will be among her possibilities, mind.'

Maitlin gave a slight smile and walked over to the car. Harris watched him drive away and headed towards the police station. As he turned the corner and started down the hill, he saw Roger Barnett striding towards him.

'Heard there was some trouble,' said Barnett. 'Thought you might need some help.'

'Well, I don't,' replied the inspector, not breaking stride.

'I just thought that—'

'And if you ever fuck up one of my operations again I'll rip your head off and shit down the hole.'

'What?' Barnett looked at him in amazement.

'I heard what you did when I asked Gallagher to stop that bus. Damned fool reckless it was, Roger, damned fool. This is no place for glory boys and you had better remember that. Folks are enough on edge without idiots like you stirring things up even further.'

'But—'

'Oh, fuck off, Roger. My friend is lying dead on a mortuary slab and I have no time for crap like this.'

'Now hang on a minute, Hawk—'

'And don't call me Hawk,' said Harris, turning and striding back down the hill. 'Only people I respect call me Hawk. Just be warned. Jerk my chain again and you'll wish you'd never come back here.'

Barnett stood in brooding silence and watched the inspector stride down the hill and up the police station steps. As the inspector walked into reception, Gallagher was chatting to the desk clerk.

'What on earth was that all about?' asked the sergeant, seeing Harris. 'Did I really see Henry Maitlin scrapping in the street?'

'You did.'

'You put him right, I take it?' said the sergeant as they walked up the stairs.

'Yes, but he tried to tell me that Barry Gough did not appreciate the sacrifices that had been made in the name of free speech.'

'He's right, surely.'

'Course he is,' chuckled Harris as they reached the top of

the stairs, 'but Henry seems to have forgotten that I know that he spent World War II in the Pay Corps. The only injury he ever picked up was a paper cut.'

And still laughing at his own joke, the inspector headed off in the direction of his office.

With the grey light of day fading rapidly to night, Rob Mackey guided the Range Rover into a lay-by on the deserted country road. For a few seconds, he sat and watched the rushing of the headlights on the nearby motorway. Behind him were the dark shapes of the northern hills and he felt, for the first time since he had left, a pang of remorse. Mackey thought of his home. Laurel House would be all warm light now. He loved it when it was like that. Loved the smell of cooking, loved the aroma of fresh coffee, loved the sound of his daughter's music wafting down from her room. Mackey smiled at the thought but it was only momentary. He supposed that they must have found his letter by now, realized that he had thrown everything away.

His phone rang and he glanced down at the screen glowing green in the darkness of the car. Liz, it said. The fifth time. For a few moments, Mackey considered answering it then shook his head, hit the cancel call button and edged the Range Rover out of the lay-by. No other vehicles were around so when he reached the roundabout, he held the vehicle on the brake, entertaining thoughts of turning back. Back to the hills. Back to Laurel House. Back to his family. He did not need to run. He could sort it all out, he told himself. Perhaps Liz would forgive him if he told her that he had made a mistake? Maybe he could talk his way out of trouble with the police? The more he thought about it, running made no sense. A smart lawyer would doubtless be able to engineer a way out. But these were only fleeting thoughts and Mackey shook his head, gunned the engine and drove across the roundabout onto the motorway filter road. The southbound carriageway of the M6 was empty; Rob Mackey's road ahead was clear and he jammed his foot on the accelerator.

CHAPTER THIRTEEN

The air was heavy and oppressive in the interview room early that evening as Jack Harris and Matty Gallagher stared across the desk at a bedraggled Lenny Portland. The petty thief's cheek was grazed and there was the beginnings of a bruise above his right eye.

'I'm gonna make a complaint,' said Portland belligerently, touching his cheek. 'Look what she did to me. Assaulted me, that's what she did.'

'You *were* running away from her at the time,' said Harris blandly. 'As I understand it, Constable Butterfield was merely doing her duty. I mean, you were not exactly acting like Mr Innocent, were you, Lenny?'

'It was that lunatic Barnett, he got me frightened, bellowing like that on the bus. I thought he was going to lamp me one. It wouldn't be the first time.'

'No? When did that happen then?'

'First time was just after he got sent back up here. I were pissing up against the church wall and he gave me a smack.' Portland raised a hand to his head again. 'Hurt, it did. And he did it again a few weeks later when I were drunk one night.'

'That's terrible.'

'Yeah, sure is, Mr Harris.' Portland nodded. 'Glad you agree with me.'

'I certainly do. Slapping people around is my job.'

The smile faded from Portland's face. 'Anyway,' he said, standing up, 'I reckon I've got a case for police harassment against you lot. In fact, I'm gonna do it right now and—'

'Sit down,' said Harris sharply.

Portland hesitated but one look at the inspector's expression was enough. Being smacked by Roger Barnett and getting on the wrong end of Jack Harris were entirely different things and Portland knew it. Everyone in the valley knew it. He sat down.

'See, Lenny,' said the inspector, 'I am not sure that you are in much of a position to get shirty with us. Trouble you're in.'

'What do you mean?'

'Recognize either of these guys?' Harris reached for the brown file lying on the table and slid out a couple of faxed photographs.

'Never seen them before in me life.'

'Look again,' said Harris, jabbing a finger on the pictures. 'If it helps, the one on the left is Dave Forrest and the one on the right is a toerag called Ronny Michaels. They're from Manchester. Ever been to Manchester, Lenny?'

'Saw Carlisle play at City's ground once. Rubbish pies.' Portland smiled; he was pleased with the quip.

'What do you think people will say when they hear that you might have been involved in the death of Harold Leach?' said Harris. Once again, the smile froze on Portland's face. 'Knowing the folks round here, Lenny, you'll be strung up from the nearest lamppost, I reckon.'

Portland looked worried. 'But I told you,' he said quickly, 'I don't know nothing about what happened to Harold. I were in the village seeing me aunt.'

'Maybe you were,' said Harris, extracting another piece of paper from the file but not showing it to Portland. 'Maybe you weren't. See, this is a witness statement which one of our officers took in Chapel Hill this afternoon.'

'Who's it from?'

'You know we don't play that game, Lenny. Suffice to say that this person had occasion to be up early in the morning and guess what he saw?'

Portland shrugged. 'Dunno,' he said. 'I weren't there, if that's what you're trying to make out.'

'Not so sure about that. See, our witness saw a man at the bottom of Harold Leach's street. About the time Harold was murdered, in fact. And guess what? Our witness gave a very good description. Sounded just like you.'

Gallagher looked sharply at the inspector but said nothing.

'You're bluffing,' said Portland, noticing the sergeant's look. 'Even Mr Gallagher here don't believe it. He must have got it wrong, this feller of yours. Perhaps he saw someone else. I weren't anywhere near Chapel Hill last night and that's a fact.'

'Then where were you?' asked Harris.

'I were in the pub all night. Left after the last bus and went straight home. I were far too drunk to get mesel' to Chapel Hill. I got witnesses as will say I were there.'

'And which pub was this, Lenny?'

'Eh?'

'The pub,' said Harris. 'Which pub was it?'

'Er, the Duck.'

'Funny, that,' said Harris, glancing at Gallagher, who seemed more comfortable now. 'We reckoned you might say that – it's your favourite strategy, I'm told – so the good sergeant here checked with the landlord and, surprise, surprise, no one can remember seeing you in there last night.'

Portland hesitated then clicked his fingers. 'Yeah, that were the night before. Sorry, Mr Gallagher, I meant the Queen's ...'

'They had not seen you either,' said the sergeant.

'In fact,' said Harris, 'we checked them all and last night

would appear to have been a historic one because you did not turn up at any of them to drink your brains out. A job which, judging from this little performance, you have already done pretty effectively.'

'I don't know what you mean. I were definitely—'

'Cut the crap, Lenny,' said Harris, leaning forward and tapping the photographs. 'Want to know what I think? I think when I saw you in the village yesterday afternoon you were casing out Harold Leach's cottage for these two and I reckon you came back with them last night.'

Portland shook his head vigorously. 'That's wrong, Mr Harris, I weren't there. Honest.'

'Our forensics reckon that three people got into the cottage and I think you were one of them.' Harris shook his head sadly. 'A frail old chap and they killed him in cold blood. Despicable behaviour, Lenny, despicable.'

'Well, it weren't me!'

'Ah, but I think it was.' Harris jabbed the pictures of the men again. 'I think you told them about this old fellow with a VC worth a few bob and I think you led them to the cottage.' Harris looked at Portland's green jumper. 'And the funny thing is, our forensics guys found a fibre the same colour as that. Fancy that, eh?'

Portland swallowed nervously.

'Harold's blood is on your hands, Lenny,' said Harris, sitting back and crossing his arms. 'My friend's blood is on your hands so now really is the time to tell us where you were.'

Silence settled on the room and Harris and Gallagher let it lengthen, the inspector toying idly with his papers, the sergeant seeming to be fascinated by the loose button on his jacket. Before the officers had gone into the interview, the sergeant had openly expressed grave doubts about the involvement of Lenny Portland, still seeing him as a petty thief unlikely to find himself embroiled in murder, but now he was having second thoughts. Gallagher looked at Harris, whose face showed no emotion. The sergeant knew what his colleague was thinking: trust my instincts, Matty lad, he was thinking, always trust my instincts. Noticing Harris watching him, the inspector gave the slightest of smiles. As the silence deepened, Lenny Portland looked at the detectives.

'He were dead when I found him,' he said in a voice so quiet the officers could hardly hear it.

Gallagher started. Harris sat forward.

'What did you say?' he asked.

'He were dead when I found him,' repeated Portland, his voice a little louder. He sounded desperate. 'Your witness were right, Mr Harris, I were in Chapel Hill last night – but I never killed him, you got to believe that. I'd never do a thing like that.'

'What were you doing there then?' asked Gallagher with a harsh edge to his voice; he was not going to make the same mistake twice. 'Come on, Lenny, what were you doing in the cottage? Time to tell us exactly what happened last night.'

'I went for the medal, all right.' Portland had gone pale and was talking quickly now. 'I admit that. I seen him wearing it in that television programme and I reckoned it must be worth a bob or two, like you said. Then when I seen him with it at that memorial thing yesterday, well, I decided to nick it. But I never meant to hurt him. Just wanted to get the medal and get out of there. I ain't never hurt no one, you know that. You have to believe that, Mr Gallagher.'

'I have no idea what to believe,' said the sergeant.

'Did you have a customer for it?' asked Harris. 'Someone you knew would fence it?'

Portland hesitated.

'Come on,' said Harris. 'We're not daft, Lenny. We know you could not have done this on your own. You were hardly going to take it down the church's car boot sale, were you now? You must have had someone. Am I right?'

117

Portland did not reply. Harris glanced at Gallagher.

'Looks like he wants to take the rap all on his own,' said the inspector. 'Sad, really, because I don't reckon Lenny meant for the old fellow to die. What do you reckon, Sergeant?'

'I reckon that if he told us who set him up to do this, it might play well with a judge.' Gallagher looked at Portland. 'Come on, son, we really do need a name.'

Portland still hesitated.

'And we need it now,' said Harris.

'Rob Mackey.'

Gallagher closed his eyes. Harris noticed the gesture and gave a barely noticeable smile before returning his attention to Portland.

'How come he wanted it?' asked Harris.

'If I tell you, I am out of trouble?'

'Depends what you tell us.'

'He's taken other things from me in the past.' Portland seemed eager to admit everything now.

'What kind of things?'

'I conned my way into some old bloke's home one time, down in Cafforth, and got away with a couple of medals from his kitchen drawer. Mackey gave me twenty quid for them. And I did another job, same thing.'

'When?'

'A couple of summers ago. This old bloke was in his back garden so I snuck in through the front and took it from his living room. That was in Ellerby, that one.'

'And Mackey paid you for that one as well?' asked Harris.

'Yeah. It weren't much, mind. Gave me a tenner. I don't like doing it really. Don't seem right to steal things from war heroes.'

'It didn't seem to stop you last night, though.'

'Yeah, well, I were skint.'

'But you didn't kill Harold Leach?'

Portland shook his head.

'No,' he said, 'no, I didn't. God's honest truth, Mr Harris.' He looked at the pictures on the desk. 'And I don't know who them men are either.'

'So when did you get to Chapel Hill?'

'About two, maybe a bit later. I was real nervous. Waited for ages until I was sure the old chap would be really deep asleep....'

'Were you alone?' asked Gallagher.

'Yeah.'

'What happened when you got to the cottage?' asked Gallagher.

'Someone had already forced the back door.'

'But you went in all the same?'

'Nearly didn't. Must have stood there five minutes making me mind up. When I got in there, into the front room, it were like a bomb had hit it. Chairs turned over, things like that. I should have got out then but something made me go upstairs to the bedroom ...' Portland's voice tailed off and he shook his head. 'Shouldn't have. Stupid thing to do.'

'And then?' asked Harris. 'What happened then, Lenny?'

'I went into the bedroom.' Portland's voice was tremulous now and he was fighting strong emotions. He looked at the inspector through dark eyes. 'It were horrible. I couldn't see much at first then I saw him, lying next to the bed. His face was all bashed in and there was blood everywhere. I can't get the image out of me head, Mr Harris. I hightailed it out of there after that. Couldn't get out fast enough.'

'And the medal? Did you take the medal with you?'

'Nah. I reckoned it were gone anyway. I reckon that's what whoever broked in was there for. The place was a right mess, like they'd been looking for it.'

'What did you do after you left the cottage?'

'Walked back to Levton Bridge. I were shaking, I can tell you.' Portland started to cry. 'You got to believe me, I did not kill him. I would never do anything like that.'

Harris sat back in his chair and surveyed Portland for a few seconds.

'I believe you,' said the inspector, glancing at a surprised Gallagher. 'As the good sergeant here keeps reminding me, murder is not really your style.'

A relieved Lenny Portland having been returned to the cells, Matty Gallagher walked slowly up the dimly lit stairs and headed for the deserted CID room where he sat down at his computer. The sergeant took his notebook from his pocket and opened it at his notes from the interview with Portland. He tapped on his keyboard. Ten minutes later he walked, deep in thought, along the corridor to the inspector's office.

'You sure about this?' asked Gallagher as he entered to find Harris tipping back in his chair with his feet up on the desk and his eyes closed. The dogs were curled up by the radiator in the corner of the room. 'You still want me to release him? I mean, you've already taken one big gamble tonight.'

'Meaning?' Harris did not look at his sergeant nor did he open his eyes.

'Telling him the witness had picked him out,' said Gallagher, picking up the delivery driver's statement from the desk. 'It could have been anyone and well you know it. It was dodgy to say the least.'

'Got to take a punt sometimes, Matty lad.' Harris returned his feet to the ground and looked at the sergeant. 'Oh, don't look like that – don't tell me that you didn't push the boat out at some time in your career? They never pulled a stroke like that down in Da Smoke?'

'Yeah, OK, maybe,' said the sergeant grudgingly. 'Nevertheless, to just let him walk out of here after he'd said all that.'

'If it makes you feel any better you can let him stew for another half hour but then I want him kicked out. He had nothing to do with the murder and you know it. If nothing else, we can charge him with the jobs he admitted to. Be good for the clear-up rate.'

'Not sure you can even do that. It's the same as with that piece of paper Esther gave you. There's no indication that any of these medals were stolen. Lenny Portland's a born liar, if you ask me. Said it to drop Mackey in it.'

'Why do you think I'm releasing him?' said Harris, walking over to stare out of the window into the darkness of the night. 'And much as it grieves me to say it, I am not sure I believe his claims about Mackey.'

'You reckon we're being sold a pup?'

'It just does not sound right. It would be interesting to see what Mackey says. Any word?'

'Nothing yet. He must have been spooked by something, mind. Maybe he knew we were talking to Lenny. Maybe he saw us lifting him off the bus. You have to admit, it's not exactly the actions of an innocent man. Then there's that weird note to his wife and kid. He'd done something wrong, he said. Maybe Lenny is right, maybe Mackey is tied up in Harold's murder somehow.'

Harris turned round. 'Maybe but we should not forget our friends from Manchester in all of this. Murdering an old man for his medal is much more their style, I would have said. Anything else on the car traffic stopped yesterday?'

'As we expected, false documents, false plate. Oh, while I remember, the pathologist says he'll do a full PM tomorrow but at first glance he can't see anything to suggest he died from anything else than the beating.'

A couple of minutes later, Gallagher was walking down

the corridor when Butterfield appeared at the top of the stairs.

'He around?' she asked the sergeant.

'Er, yeah. In his office.' He looked hard at the constable as she walked past, head down. 'You OK, pet?'

'Been better.'

'Can't be as bad as me,' said Gallagher. 'I let Rob Mackey slip through my fingers.'

'You wouldn't believe what I've been doing with him.'

Without elaborating on the comment, Butterfield headed for the inspector's office. Gallagher watched her go in bemusement then turned to head for the canteen. He had a sudden yearning for a bacon sandwich. As he entered the room, his mobile phone rang. The sergeant glanced down at the name on the screen – Jules, it said.

'Hi, love,' he said in the phone. 'You on duty yet?'

'Yeah. Looks like it'll be a busy one – already had a couple of heart attacks. Oh, and two drunks brought in after a fight.'

'We had Henry Maitlin brawling up here.'

'What? The old duffer?'

'Yeah,' chuckled Gallagher, 'scrapping away with Barry Gough, he was. Last thing we want.'

'Yeah, folks have been a bit funny for days.'

'Don't you start. I've had enough of that from Harris.'

'The radio said you haven't got anyone for your murder.'

'I'm afraid not,' said Gallagher, walking up to the counter where he smiled at the assistant. 'A bacon butty, please, Edie. Actually, make that two.'

'Fat bastard,' said his wife's voice down the phone.

Matty Gallagher smiled. It was the first time he could remember smiling in a long time.

Back down the corridor, Jack Harris was sitting at his desk, sifting through the day's reports, when Butterfield knocked lightly on the door.

'Ah, Constable, how goes it?' he said, gesturing to the chair. 'Pull up a pew. You've worked hard today, you must be knackered. I understand you showed some nifty rugby skills when you brought Lenny Portland down.'

'I guess so.' Butterfield sat down heavily on one of the chairs.

'Why the long face?' asked Harris. 'We'll crack this one. Just a matter of time.'

'I am afraid I have something to tell you, and you are not going to like it. And I mean really not like it.'

Thirty minutes later, Jack Harris was alone in his office again, sitting staring into the middle distance, fingers pressed together in a praying motion. Occasionally, he sighed and at one he point closed his eyes. After a few minutes, he murmured 'silly girl'. Scoot looked up from his spot next to the radiator.

'It does make you wonder,' said Harris. 'I mean, it really does. What was she thinking of? Don't answer that, Scoot, I think we all know the answer to that one.'

Scoot ambled across the room and rubbed his head against the inspector's leg. Seeing what was happening, Archie did the same.

'And don't either of you get any daft ideas,' said Harris as he scratched both of them behind the ear in turn.

The inspector's reverie was disturbed by the ringing of his mobile phone. He walked over to where his jacket was hanging on a peg on the wall and took out the device. Glancing down at the screen, Harris smiled. Leckie, it said.

'You got something for me?' asked the inspector into the phone. 'Because believe me I could do with something.'

'Just got a call from our DI. Your two guys Forrest and Michaels? Standish says they're back in Manchester.'

'He got them in custody?'

'Not yet. One of our informants saw them leaving a pub in the town centre but they have gone to ground. I take it you are still after them?'

'Too right I am,' said Harris, returning to sit once more with his feet up on the desk. 'The way it's looking they're my best bet for the old guy's murder.'

'Well, like I said, you want anything solving you just give me a ring, old son. Listen, Jamie Standish was wondering if you wanted to come down here?'

'He was?'

'Yeah, I was gobsmacked when he made the offer. Thought you would be the last person he would want to see. After … well, you know.'

'I know,' said Harris.

'Anyway, he's pretty sure they'll turn up in one of their other haunts before long. He thought you might like to be there when it happens?'

'Sounds good,' said Harris. 'Can I bring someone down with me?'

'You can bring that pretty constable with you, if you like.'

'I think,' said Harris, 'that she has done more than enough for one day.'

Shortly before nine o'clock, the main door to Levton Bridge Police Station opened and Lenny Portland walked out into the damp night air. After glancing along the deserted street, he headed up the hill, bound for the welcoming warmth of the market place's pubs. Portland had just rounded the corner when a man stepped out from a back alley running down the side of the Co-op, barring his way.

'What do you want?' muttered Portland, making as if to brush past him.

'Heard the cops pulled you in,' said the man, catching his arm and not allowing him to pass. 'You better be telling the truth about not being involved in the old feller's murder.'

'I am.'

'Then what you been saying? Better not have mentioned me. I don't want dragging into it.'

'I said nowt about you.' Portland shrugged his arm free.

'Then what did you tell Harris?' The man's voice was anxious. 'I assume it was Harris?'

'Yeah, him and that Gallagher bloke. I would rather it had been that Butterfield bird – she's nice, she is. Anyway, stop looking so worried. I told them that I was working for Mackey.'

'You did what? I thought we agreed that you would not say anything.'

'They were really heavy,' said Portland plaintively.

'Heavy?' asked the man, peering at the gash on his cheek. 'That how you got that?'

'Nah, that's when that blonde detective knocked me over.'

'Tough man, aren't we?' said the man sarcastically. 'So they didn't lay a hand on you?'

'Nah.'

'So why tell them it was Mackey, for God's sake?'

'They had a witness what saw me in the village last night. I had to say something and Mackey was the first thing that came into my mind. Everyone knows that Harris hates him. Don't look like that. I had to say something. Harris, he said that I was in the frame for murdering the old guy if I didn't come up with something.'

'But you didn't mention me?'

Portland shook his head vigorously. 'I wouldn't drop you in it, mate. I ain't like that.'

'You dropped Mackey in it and he's done nothing wrong. What did Harris make of it?' The man glanced nervously round as he saw a woman walking her dog on the far side of the market place.

'Seemed happy with it.'

The man watched the woman disappear into a side alley then nodded.

'It might not be so bad,' he said. 'Harris would believe anything about Mackey. Yeah, maybe it's not too bad. I'm down at the storehouse tomorrow anyway so I should be able to keep out of Harris's way. Already had one run-in with him.'

'Can I go now?'

'Yeah, go on.' Portland had only taken three steps when the man grabbed his arm. 'But just remember, if my name gets dragged into this ...'

'I'll remember.' Portland nodded, wriggling free and heading across the market place. 'How could I forget? Jesus, I need a drink.'

'Well, just keep your trap shut if you get drunk. You know what you're like when you're in your cups.'

'I will,' said Portland. 'I promise.'

Having seen him go into a nearby pub, the man walked out of the market place, not noticing the dark figure shrinking back into the shadows, watching him in silence. When the man had gone, Detective Constable James Larch stepped out onto the pavement and started following at a reasonable distance, his surveillance eventually coming to a stop in a terraced street where his quarry let himself into a house. Leaning against a wall at the end of the street and watching as the downstairs light went on, Larch fished his mobile out of his pocket and dialled a number.

'Gallagher,' said the voice on the other end.

'It's me. Look, I hope you don't mind, Sarge, but I changed the plan a bit.'

'For why?'

'Well, Portland has gone into the Duck and experience suggests it will be a long time before he comes out.'

'Granted,' said the sergeant, who was in the CID squad room. 'So what's the change of plan?'

'I followed Barry Gough instead.'

'Why on earth would you do that?'

'I saw something rather interesting in the market place. Our friend Gough would appear to have plenty to discuss with Lenny Portland.'

'Didn't know they knocked around together. Lenny's never shown much interest in pacifism,' said Gallagher. 'Not sure he could even spell it.'

Larch gave a low laugh. 'I reckon you're right,' he said, 'but I kinda got the impression that it wasn't about that. They seemed to be having a really intense conversation and when they went their separate ways, Gough grabbed him by the arm. Looked like he was really hurting Portland. Portland couldn't get away quick enough.'

'Now that is interesting. Where's Gough now then?'

'He's gone home. Number 15 Raymond Street's his gaff, I think?'

'Scruffy place, peeling green paint, loads of posters in the window?'

'That's the one. What do you want me to do? Go back and keep an eye on Portland? Can't really go into the Duck, he'll clock me straightaway, but I could wait outside.'

'No,' said the sergeant. 'No, I reckon we've got enough to do without hanging around outside pubs.'

'But I thought the governor wanted me to—'

'You leave Harris to me,' said Gallagher. 'He's not here anyway. He's on his way to Manchester. The glamour of high command, Jimmy boy, the glamour of command.'

'You ever been to Manchester?' asked Larch.

'No.'

'Went to see Carlisle play City one time. Crap pies.'

'Now where have I heard that before?' said Gallagher.

A weary Rob Mackey pulled the Range Rover off the motorway shortly after nine and edged it into the motel car park. After reaching onto the back seat for his overnight bag, he got out and walked over to the reception.

'Good evening, sir,' said a pleasant young woman as he pushed open the door and walked up to the counter. 'How can I help?'

'A room for the night.'

'Certainly, sir.' She busied herself with the paperwork. 'Have you come far today, sir?'

'Too far,' said Mackey.

The girl looked at him with bemusement but he did not elaborate on the comment so she went back to her work. As he waited, Mackey's mobile phone rang. He took it out of his jacket pocket and looked down at the illuminated screen. Liz, it said. The thirteenth time she had called. He had listened to one of her messages but had stopped before the end, tiring of his wife's angry tirades. He had not listened to any of the others.

'Don't mind me, sir,' said the girl as it continued to ring. 'It might be important.'

Mackey slipped the phone back into his pocket as it stopped ringing.

'No,' he said, 'no, I don't think it is.'

The girl had just finished filling out the paperwork when Mackey's phone went again. He ignored it and it stopped ringing. A matter of seconds later, it rang again. Mackey sighed and took the phone out again, glancing at the screen. Al, it said.

'You're popular, sir,' said the girl brightly, handing over his credit card and his booking form.

Mackey gave a slight smile.

'How right you are,' he said, picking up his bag and heading towards the stairs. 'Just with all the wrong people.'

The fog was rolling thick and silent over the northern hills as Jack Harris guided the Land Rover carefully across the moor, occasionally leaning over the steering wheel as he struggled to make out the way ahead. Visibility had been poor ever since he and Detective Inspector Gillian Roberts had pulled away from the police station half an hour before, leaving the dogs in the doting care of the two women in the control room. Roberts, sitting in silence beside Harris, not speaking in order to let him concentrate on the road, was Levton Bridge's only detective inspector. A mother of two in her early fifties, she affected a matronly demeanour but behind the avuncular façade was an officer as tough and sharp as they came, one who thrived on the challenges of the job. Her eyes gleamed in the darkness; this was the kind of thing she loved most. Her daily life tended to be spent dealing with the likes of Lenny Portland so the prospect of coming up against more serious villains had her excited.

As he drove, Jack Harris was experiencing similar emotions. That he still did so five years after leaving Manchester never failed to surprise him. He had always assumed that he would be able to adapt completely to life back in the valley, that he had seen enough major-league crime during his time in the city to be sated. An officer who had always appreciated working in Manchester, who had always felt a rush of adrenaline when the big jobs were on, who relished bumping heads with villains, he had nevertheless assumed that his decision to seek out more peaceful climes would always seem like the right one. By and large it had been but on nights like this, when the chase was on, Jack Harris felt a call to his previous life.

The inspector knew that he had to resist such moments; deep in his heart he did not want to go back to Manchester. He had felt claustrophobic living in the city, like he could hear everyone's thoughts. He had known then, knew now, that the northern hills would keep calling to him until he finally committed his life fully to them; it was, he had reasoned, rather like a marriage and the hills were his ever-constant partner. And one on which he could rely to be faithful. Nevertheless, as ever in such situations as this, when the paradox of his emotions were so clearly exposed, the inspector felt the stirrings of excitement.

As the fog cleared at last and the road began to dip, the detectives could see the twinkling lights of villages spread out across the flatlands ahead of them, and in the far distance the town of Roxham, the area's largest community. They would turn off long before they reached it, though, the Land Rover heading for the M6 southbound. As Harris relaxed and sat back in his seat again, Roberts glanced across at him.

'This Ronny Michaels character,' she said. 'You know him of old then?'

'From my Manchester days. A job on the M62. There was a lorry driver parked up in a truck stop for the night. Carrying crates of lager. Michaels and his gang jumped him when he nipped out to check his fastenings. We'd had a few jobs like that over the previous few months – same gang, we reckoned. Michaels coshed the driver. Landed him in hospital.'

'Nice lad. How did you get them?'

'Ah, well, because there had been quite a few of the jobs,

we had been running an op so when the call came in, everyone was on standby. Traffic had a couple of fast cars parked near where it happened and intercepted them as they tried to get away. They tried to outrun them but not sure a loaded Ford Transit had much chance against one of our vehicles. They do like the glory stuff, the traffic boys.'

'Rather like our Mr Barnett,' said Roberts.

'You heard about that then?'

'It's all anyone's talking about. He's walking round like he's some kind of hero. From what Matty says the bus would have exploded if it had got above fifteen miles an hour. Not sure Barnett needed to do the high-speed pursuit stuff. Matty's well hacked off.'

'I'm sure he is.' Harris frowned. 'I lost it with Roger, if I'm honest. Threatened him.'

'Why on earth did you do that?'

'I'm really struggling with this,' sighed Harris. He looked across at her with dark eyes. 'I really am.'

'Because it's Harold?'

'Yeah, because it's Harold. We had known each other for years. Since I was a kid. First time I met him I must have been, I don't know, ten, eleven, and I was out on the moor when I saw him walking towards me. Pointed out a buzzard to me on the horizon. All I could see was a black speck but he knew that it was a female and what it had had for breakfast. We got talking and we'd been friends ever since. He taught me so much about wildlife, you know. I've lost a friend, Gillian.'

'You sure you want to handle the inquiry? I am sure they would send another—'

'No, I'll be fine.'

'Sure? I mean, just because you were upset is not a reason to take it out on Roger Barnett.'

'He deserved it. Not sure whether to take it any further, mind.'

'In my experience, a hard word from Jack Harris usually suffices,' she said with a smile. 'Why the worried look, Jack? You think Barnett will complain? He'd be stupid if he did.'

'Who knows? And wouldn't Curtis love it if he did? He's been waiting for something like that. Let's not talk about it any more. Just gets me narked.'

'Fair enough. You were saying. This lot that did over the lorry driver. What happened?'

'Well, we had them bang to rights and they knew it. We found the cosh in the back of the van along with dozens of crates that they had taken from the lorry.'

'Nice job.'

'Yeah, and what's more,' said Harris, grinning, 'the halfwit behind the wheel had already had two cans of Special. Not only did we get him for robbery but traffic breathalyzed him and he blew positive. Kept the traffic boys happy.'

Roberts laughed. It was always good when Harris lightened up. It just didn't happen often enough, in her view.

'And you were the one who interviewed Michaels, I take it?' she said.

'Yeah.' Harris nodded as he guided the Land Rover round a sharp bend. 'It was my op so I did them all. He admitted being involved in the job straightaway, put his hands up to another four as well, but he swore blind that he never hit the driver. Claimed it was one of the others. He seemed genuinely concerned about what had happened to the guy. Never did work out if he was a coward or a villain with a conscience.'

'Which one did you come up with?'

'A twat.'

'Ah,' said Gillian Roberts.

'Now this is interesting,' said Gallagher, turning away from the computer screen, tipping back in his chair and glancing at Butterfield, who was sitting in the far corner of the CID room, staring out of the window. 'There's nothing on Mackey but we may have something on—'

'There's something you need to know,' she said, turning to look at him.

'You've been dobbing Rob Mackey.'

'What?' She stared at him in amazement.

'Just a wild guess,' said Gallagher with an impish look on his face. 'It was that or you were a Martian.'

'Who told you?' Butterfield said angrily.

'Saw your spaceship parked in the yard.' Noticing that she was not laughing, he added. 'Harris.'

'But I told him it was a personal matter.'

'The DCI would beg to differ. He sees it as an operational matter and one I needed to know about. For what it's worth, I think he's right. I mean, your pal Mackey has got a lot of questions to answer, has he not?'

'I guess,' she said glumly. 'To his wife for a start.'

'Indeed.'

'What else did Harris say?'

'That he would have liked to have known about your dalliance a bit earlier. Why didn't you tell him, for God's sake, Alison? You knew Mackey was a part of the Morritt investigation. Surely you must have seen that there was a conflict of interest?'

'But your inquiries showed Rob did nothing wrong. Besides, we got together after you finished your investigation.'

'But before the inquest. At least if you had told the governor you would have covered your back if things went funny.'

'I didn't think he'd approve,' said Butterfield, turning back to stare out of the window. 'I just didn't think he would approve.'

'What, and you think he does now?' said Gallagher sharply. Noticing her unhappy expression, he added in a softer voice, 'Look, love, I just think the DCI does not like these kind of things being kept from him. You know what he's like with surprises. Surely you have not forgotten the fiasco when we tried to throw the curmudgeonly old bastard a birthday party?'

'But there's no law against what I've done, Matty.' She sounded plaintive when she said it, looking at Gallagher as if seeking approbation for what she had done.

'The DCI's view is that it shows a lack of judgement. Look, I know you like Mackey but in my view the man's a prat. One, might I remind you, who tried to block the DCI's investigation when that flipping bird was shot. And one who is now up to his neck in a murder inquiry.'

'I'm sure it's all a misunderstanding. Rob's not so bad when you get to know him. He can be quite gentle.'

'You,' said the sergeant with a twinkle in his eye, 'would know more about that than me.'

The comment eased the tension in the room and Butterfield shied the phone book at him. Gallagher ducked, roaring with laughter as he did so.

'Bastard!' she said. 'You are a complete bastard!'

'I like to think so,' said Gallagher, grinning.

Their hilarity was interrupted by the arrival of Roger Barnett, who strode into the room and looked round.

'This how you go about solving a murder inquiry then?' he asked. 'Your gaffer ain't in his office. Where is he?'

'Not in his office,' said Gallagher, winking at Butterfield.

'Don't come the funny man with me. I asked where your—'

'Where our governor is has nothing to do with you,' said Gallagher, bridling at the sergeant's tone of voice. 'What do you want him for anyway?'

'He bawled me out earlier – threatened me, he did – and I want him to apologize.'

'Apologize? Jack Harris?'

'Yeah, Jack Harris. I was going to take it straight to Curtis then I thought, no, if I get an apol—'

'Not sure you'll get an apology from our gaffer,' said Gallagher. 'In fact, he's more likely to ask you why you've been knocking Lenny Portland about.'

'What?'

'That's what Lenny seems to think.'

'He got what he deserved!'

'And so, I imagine, will you if you try it on with our governor. I know they do things differently in the buzzing metropolis that is Roxham but up here Jack Harris's word is law. Always worth bearing that in mind, Roger. What do you think, Constable?'

Butterfield nodded. 'Oh, aye,' she said. 'Law, Roger.'

Barnett stalked angrily from the room.

'You just wait,' he said over his shoulder. 'You just see what Curtis thinks to all of this.'

'Yeah, good luck with that,' shouted Gallagher. He frowned. 'Don't know why we're laughing. This could be what Curtis has been waiting for.'

'The DCI's a survivor.'

'So was Harold Leach,' said Gallagher, walking out of the room. 'And look what happened to him.'

Harris guided the Land Rover up the motorway slip road and onto the largely empty southbound carriageway. As he did so, his dashboard-mounted mobile phone rang.

'Harris,' he said reaching down to press the receive call button.

'It's Leckie,' said the voice at the other end. 'You on the way down here?'

'Yeah, just pulling onto the M6. Why?'

'Just had the DI on. One of our informants reckon your two guys may turn up at a pub on one of our housing estates. It's notorious for stoppy-backs and, apparently, they sometimes make an appearance on a Thursday night. Been doing it for months. Nice of our informant not to tell us before. We didn't even know they were back in town.'

'Perhaps they were waiting until some professional coppers turned up.'

'Yeah, never know when you're likely to need someone who knows about sheep in Manchester,' said Leckie. 'Place is thick with the buggers, you know.'

'Should we head direct to the pub then?'

'No, I'll text you the details of where to find us. Did you take my advice and bring that delightful little blonde constable with you?'

Before Harris could reply, Gillian Roberts leaned over towards the phone.

"Fraid not, Graham,' she said in her best matronly tone. 'He brought her wrinkled old granny instead.'

All they heard was a low laugh from Leckie.

CHAPTER SIXTEEN

Gallagher joined Butterfield at the squad-room window and they watched as four police vans and two patrol cars edged their way out of the station yard and onto the main road outside the station.

'That's the governor's doing,' said Gallagher. 'He asked for a show of force to reassure folks. That last thing we want is another incident a couple of days before Remembrance Sunday.'

Butterfield did not reply and silence settled on the room. Gallagher hesitated.

'I take it,' he said, without looking at her, 'that you did not know anything about what Mackey was up to?'

'Do you even have to ask?' she replied sharply.

'I had to, though. I mean, didn't I? Oh, don't look like that. I imagine the governor said the same thing.'

'Firstly,' she said with anger in her voice as she stared hard at him, 'there's not much to suggest exactly what Rob's done, if he's done anything at all, and secondly, do you really think I would have stayed with him if I had known? I mean, do you, Matty? Knowing he could have been mixed up with something like this?'

'No, no, I don't think you would.'

'I'm glad.' There was an awkward silence. The constable broke it. 'Anyway, what were you saying before Barnett interrupted us?'

'Oh, yeah,' said Gallagher, relieved that the tension had eased. He walked back to his computer. 'See, I had this crazy idea that Rob might be advertising his stuff on the web – ebay, something like that, you know?'

'Curtis would be delighted if we could solve all crimes by internet,' said Butterfield, remaining at the window to watch the patrols disperse. 'Save on mileage, that would. But even if you were right that Rob is into something dodgy, I am pretty sure that he would not be so stupid to use his own name. He's a pretty smart cookie, you know.'

'I guessed that but we have his contact numbers so I thought I would try them anyway. Long shot, I know.' Gallagher tapped the computer screen. 'Anyway, you will be delighted to hear that I found nothing – well, not about Rob anyway. But guess who is dealing in war memorabilia?'

'Dunno.' she shrugged. 'Who?'

'Humour me for a moment. Think of the last person in the world you would expect?'

'Mother Teresa?'

'She's dead.'

'I don't know then. She was the obvious one.'

'Barry Gough,' said Gallagher dramatically. He tapped the computer screen. 'We had his number as well. Got it one time when he was lifted for protesting so I keyed that in. Another long shot, really, but look what came up.'

Butterfield walked over to the computer and shook her head in disbelief as she looked over his shoulder.

'You sure that's his number?' she said as she read the 'Contact Us' section of a website, which featured a series of military images and the words 'Memorabilia for Sale'. 'I always assumed he would be against anything like that on principle.'

'Clearly his views are a somewhat movable feast.'

'Hang on,' said Butterfield as Gallagher clicked back to the home page and she pointed at a piece of small print. 'That says that they do not deal in medals.'

'So it does.' He looked disappointed. 'And much as I would like to lock the little bugger up and throw away the key, I guess there's nothing illegal about what this lot are doing, as far as I can see. It's simply a bunch of saddoes selling old army gear.'

'Unless they're nicking it first.'

'Unless they're nicking it first.'

'Look,' said Butterfield, pointing to an address on the screen, 'they trade out of Manchester. What do you reckon that is – an industrial estate or something? A lock-up, perhaps?'

'If only we had someone in Manchester who could help us out,' said Gallagher, picking up the phone. 'Oh, hang on, we just happen to have a couple of our finest on their way there as we speak. I'll ring Leckie first. See what we can dig up.'

'You decided what you're going to do about young Butterfield?' asked Gillian Roberts as the Land Rover sped through the night.

'Not sure what I can do,' said the inspector, moving into the middle lane to overtake a slow-moving lorry. 'Not sure there's a law against dating a git.'

'You just do not like Rob Mackey, do you?'

'Can't stand the man.'

'And yet you are so considerate with everyone else,' she said, shooting him a sly look. 'It's so out of character.'

'That's below the belt,' said Harris but he did not seem offended by the comment.

'Talking of below the belt, do we know how long they had been sleeping together?'

'Only a few months. She did not want anyone to know about it.'

'Especially you.'

'I guess so.' He gave the slightest of smiles. 'I can't imagine why. Like you so rightly point out, I am usually so understanding.'

'Just keep your eyes on the road. Don't want to hit that flying pig if it gets too low, do we now? Talking of people with delusions of the truth, do you believe Portland? Is Rob Mackey wrapped up in this murder somehow?'

'Can't see it.'

'Then why's he done a runner?'

'Not sure. There's something we don't know and I don't like not knowing things.'

'I'll be sure to remind young Butterfield about that next time I see her.'

The inspector's mobile phone bleeped and Roberts leaned over to call up the text.

'It's a pub called the Red Lion,' she said. 'Leckie says we are to meet a DI called Jamie Standish at the main town police station and they'll take us there. Says you will be delighted to see Standish again. He's put an exclamation mark after it. What's that about then?'

'Maybe I'll tell you one day.'

'I'll hold you to that.' Roberts read to the end of the message. 'They want to know how long we'll be.'

'Not long,' said Harris, ramming his foot on the accelerator. 'Not long at all.'

'Barry Gough?' said Leckie, tapping on his own keyboard. 'Not sure I've heard of him, Matty. Why so interested? Something to do with these guys your governor is after?'

'Possibly. I hope we're not wasting your time, Graham. I don't imagine you'll find much about him.'

'Au contraire. Your Mr Gough has got quite a record. All minor disorder stuff, mind. Public order, that kind of thing.'

'Linked to war protests, no doubt.'

'Most of it. According to this, he left Manchester two years ago but no one knew where he went. Did you know he was ex-army?'

'But he's an anti-war protestor.'

'Maybe it's less to do with principle and more to do with getting his own back. Says here that he was kicked out at the age of twenty-one for being drunk on duty three times in a week. His involvement in protests would appear to have started after that.'

'What else has he been up to?'

'D and D, a bit of petty crime. He's not much of a fish, Matty. What makes you think he might be linked to the murder of your old feller?'

'He's been selling war memorabilia through a bunch in Manchester. Their website mentions an address. Sale Street.'

'Yeah, I know it. It's on the edge of town. Not much to it, mind – a few workshops, half of which are empty. In fact, I did hear the council might be knocking it down. I guess your gaffer could take a look while he's down here but it sounds like a long shot. Anything else you want me to check?'

'I'm still trying to make sense of a war protestor who ends up selling memorabilia on the QT.'

'Nothing like a man of principle.'

'And Barry Gough is nothing like a man of principle.'

'I'll set 'em up, you knock 'em in,' said Leckie.

Silence had settled on Levton Bridge market place, the only movement a cat skulking in the shadows. Shortly before the town clock chimed midnight, a police van drove slowly past the rows of shops and tearooms. The driver brought the vehicle to a halt as it drew parallel with the war memorial. He lowered his window and peered through the fog.

'Anything?' asked his colleague.

'Nah, seems OK. After all, who would be stupid enough to try something after what happened at Chapel Hill?'

'I guess,' said the passenger. 'Come on, I'm freezing, let's get a cuppa. We'll take another look a bit later. No one's going to do anything now.'

The driver nodded his agreement and the van drove round

the corner in the direction of the police station. When it had gone, a figure emerged from an alley on the far side of the market place and walked slowly towards the memorial.

Liz Mackey sat in the darkened kitchen at Laurel House and nursed her fourth glass of whisky. The mobile phone sat on the table in front of her. Its battery was starting to run low. Wearily, Liz reached out and dialled her husband's mobile number yet again and placed the phone to her ear. 'The owner of this phone is unable to take your call,' said the automated voice at the other end. It had been saying that for hours. Liz sighed and put the phone back on the table. The kitchen door opened and her teenage daughter walked into the room. She was dressed in her pyjamas. Bleary-eyed, Bethany glanced at the clock.

'It's 1.30, Mum,' she said. 'Go to bed.'

'I can't sleep. I keep thinking.'

'I know,' said Bethany, sitting down and putting her arm round her shoulder. 'So do I. Where do you think he is?'

'I have no idea. With his fancy woman, I suppose.'

'Are you sure about him having an affair? I mean, the letter that the police took, it doesn't actually say that, does it?'

'It's what it meant,' said Liz. She reached across to stroke her daughter's hair. 'I'm sorry, love.'

'For what, Mum?'

'For letting it happen.'

'Don't talk daft. The only person to blame is Dad. And the other woman. Do you know who she is?'

'I have no idea,' she said; she was slurring her words a little.

They sat in silence for a few moments.

Bethany said, 'Did you love him, Mum?'

Liz reached for the bottle as she considered the question.

'Don't you think you've had enough?' said her daughter,

moving it further away. 'God, that was virtually full this morning.'

Liz looked thoughtful. 'No,' she said, 'I don't think I do love your father. Maybe not even at the start. Is that a terrible thing to say?'

Bethany shook her head. 'Not really. I don't love him either. He gave me good reason to—'

'Please God don't tell me that he—'

'No, nothing like that, Mum,' said her daughter quickly. 'He did not have time for anyone else.'

Liz smiled sadly. 'Except for his mystery woman,' she said.

'Except for his mystery woman,' agreed Bethany, sliding the bottle over to her mother. 'Go on, have another drink, you old soak.'

Liz poured some whisky out and held the glass up.

'Here's to her,' she said. 'She's welcome to him. I hope she's happy with what she's done.'

Alison Butterfield sat in the darkened kitchen of her flat close to the market place and nursed her fourth glass of whisky. The mobile phone sat on the table in front of her. Its battery was starting to run low. Wearily, Butterfield reached out and dialled Rob Mackey's mobile number yet again and placed the phone to her ear. 'The owner of this phone is unable to take your call,' said the automated voice at the other end. It had been saying that for hours. Butterfield sighed and put the phone back on the table.

CHAPTER SEVENTEEN

The rain was falling again when Harris and Roberts parked the Land Rover outside the Manchester police station. As they got out, a tall, lean plain-clothes officer walked out from the bright lights of the reception area.

'Jamie,' said Harris as they shook hands. 'Glad they saw sense and made you DI. I told them you were a good lad.'

'I did hear that you put a word in for me. Much appreciated. Hope we may be able to return the favour tonight.'

It seemed to the watching Gillian Roberts that, for all the apparent generosity of the detective inspector's welcome, there was a lack of warmth in his utterances. A forced formality. As ever when she found herself in such situations, she wondered about the things she did not know about Jack Harris. The DCI rarely talked about his life but there had been stories, rumours, fragments that suggested a past with its fair share of dark shadings. Roberts had seen enough of her boss's methods to suspect that what worked in the rural backwater of Levton Bridge might not be so readily tolerated in the urban sprawl. She had always suspected that there had been those who had been pleased to see the DCI leave the city. Jamie Standish, she decided, had been one of them.

'Jamie, this is DI Roberts,' said Harris, gesturing to her and cutting through her reverie. 'She's part of my team at Levton Bridge.'

'Glad to meet you,' said Standish, shaking the DI's hand as well, a little less guarded this time. 'Welcome to sunny Manchester, Inspector, although we don't really have time for these niceties, mind. Your two guys have turned up at the pub.'

Twenty minutes later, the inspector's Land Rover was parked on one of the town's housing estates and Harris and Roberts were sitting and surveying a rundown pub which stood at the end of a row of dilapidated shops. The shops were in darkness but there was a pale light shining through the ragged curtains of the pub. Parked next to the Land Rover was Jamie Standish's car; they could see that the detective inspector was on the phone.

'It's at times like this,' said Harris, glancing across at the nearby houses, most of which were boarded up, 'that I remember why I left Manchester.'

'It's why I never left our force. I had the opportunity, you know. Could have joined West Yorkshire but I just couldn't work areas like this. I know we have some dodgy places back home but nothing like this.'

'It's not all this bad. Some of the area is really pleasant.'

'No hills, though.'

'No,' said Harris, 'no hills.'

'Must have been a big decision, leaving Manchester.' Roberts looked at him. 'I mean, from what I hear you were on the fast-track when you were down here.'

'Maybe. Maybe not.' Harris hesitated. 'How can I put it, Gillian? Not everyone appreciated my way of working. They were a little more PC than I am.'

Roberts looked across at Standish in his car.

'And him?' she said. 'Was he one of those who did not appreciate your way of working?'

Harris did not have chance to answer the question.

'Here we go,' he said, noticing three police vans pull up not far from the pub and disgorge a large number of officers in riot gear. As the team quickly congregated, Harris and Roberts got out of the Land Rover and joined Standish as he walked towards the pub. Another vehicle pulled up behind the vans and a couple of officers got out carrying firearms.

'We going to need them?' asked Harris.

'You can never be too careful. This isn't some backwoods village, you know.' Standish stopped walking and turned to face them. 'Let our heavy mob go in first. Leave the arrests to them.'

'Hang on, what…?'

'I don't know how you do things at Levton Bridge but here we have our own way of working.' Standish gave him a hard look. 'Understand?'

'Of course,' said Harris, having looked as if he might continue to remonstrate with him. 'It's your show, Jamie. We would not dream of interfering.'

'Just make sure you don't.' There was an awkward silence between the two men then Standish added, in what seemed to Roberts, like a forced attempt at joviality, 'After all, it wouldn't look good if we let a couple of visiting cops get themselves shot on our patch, would it?'

'Think of the paperwork,' said Harris.

'Quite.'

Seconds later, it started. One of the uniforms approached the pub door with a hydraulic ram and there was the sound of splintering wood and shouted warnings as the officers poured into the building. The detectives could hear more hollering from inside, the noise of chairs and tables being overturned and the smashing of glass. After less than a minute, a man ran out of the front door, barging his way past one of the uniformed officers, knocking him to the ground. Looking wildly about him, the man saw the detectives and started to run towards the nearby houses.

'That's Michaels,' said Harris urgently.

'You just leave him to …' began Standish but a second man

appeared from the front door of the pub, brushed past the uniformed officer, who had only just struggled to his feet, and started to run in the opposite direction to his accomplice.

'And that looks like Forrest,' said Harris, looking at Standish then at the uniformed officer in the pub doorway, who had sunk to his knees again. 'You can't get them both, Jamie. And I'm not sure chummy is going to be much help.'

Standish hesitated then nodded.

'OK,' he said reluctantly. 'You get Dave Forrest and—'

'No, I'll get Michaels,' interrupted Harris and started to chase the fleeing man.

'No tricks!' shouted Standish after him and Harris waved a hand in acknowledgment.

'Tricks?' asked Roberts.

Standish did not reply but gave a low curse beneath his breath and ran after Forrest. Gillian Roberts watched Harris closing in on Michaels then turned to follow Standish. It did not take Harris long to catch up with Ronny Michaels in a back alley a hundred metres from the pub. Breathing hard, Michaels slowed as he heard the thundering footsteps getting closer behind him. He whirled round to see the inspector bearing down on him. Michaels' eyes widened as he recognized his pursuer.

'You!' he gasped.

'Long time no see, Ronny,' said Harris, slowing down to walking pace. 'Beaten up any innocent old men lately?'

'I don't know what ...'

'I think you murdered my friend, sunshine.' Harris was battling to control his emotions. 'I think you kicked his brains in.'

'It weren't me did that, Harris,' said Michaels quickly. His eyes had widened even further and he looked scared. 'Honest. I never killed him.'

'God help you if you did.'

Noticing that the detective had clenched his fist, Michaels

gave a cry of alarm and lashed out. Harris ducked expertly beneath the blow and flicked out his hand. The punch caught Michaels on the side of the face and he staggered sideways, clattering into the fence, his knees buckling. He stayed there for a moment or two then, on seeing the inspector advance, swayed to his feet and turned to run. He did not even see the punch. The next thing Michaels knew, he was lying on his back with a pounding head and the inspector standing over him.

'It weren't me,' said Michaels desperately. He held up an arm to fend off the next blow. 'It were Dave did it.'

'Will you say that on the record?' asked Harris as Michaels scrabbled a few feet further away.

'Yeah, anything. Just don't hurt me.'

'That what Harold said? He ask you to stop hurting him as well? That what happened, Ronny?'

'No!'

Harris walked up to Michaels, stared at him for a few moments then pulled back his foot.

'Please, no!' wailed Michaels.

By the time Dave Forrest had reached the end of the row of shops, the younger and fitter Jamie Standish had already caught up with him. Hearing him closing in, Forrest turned and struck out. Standish did not read the punch in time and was sent reeling by the blow to his face, sinking to his knees as he leant against one of the shop windows, his world spinning and his stomach heaving. Forrest was about to turn and run when he saw the approaching Roberts.

'Who the hell are you?' he asked.

'I,' she said calmly, 'am DI Roberts from Levton Bridge. You know Levton Bridge, I think, Dave? Why, I believe you might even have been there yesterday.'

Forrest eyed her uncertainly, worried by her calm demeanour.

'On your way to kill Harold Leach,' she added, 'if that jogs your memory. Easy to forget these little things in the confusion of everyday life, isn't it?'

Forrest glanced over his shoulder.

'If,' said Roberts, 'you are assessing the odds of outrunning a woman who is old enough to be your mother, let me help you make your mind up.'

Before Forrest could react, the detective inspector had moved behind him, grasped his arms and snapped a pair of handcuffs round his wrists. She walked the bewildered man to where Jamie Standish was now standing up, holding his head.

'Good work,' he said ruefully. 'Jack Harris has taught you well.'

Together, they walked Forrest back to the pub where other officers were loading more men into the additional police vans that had now arrived.

'A good haul,' said Standish, eyeing them approvingly. 'We've been after a couple of them for a while now. With Michaels, that makes for a good night's work. Assuming your gaffer got him, of course.'

'He'll have got him,' said Roberts.

They heard a scream from the direction of the back alley.

'Just depends what shape he's in when he does,' replied Standish bleakly. 'Those two have history. There's a lot of people have history with your governor.'

'So it would seem,' she murmured.

The two detectives watched as Harris ushered Ronny Michaels out of the alleyway. Michaels was walking unsteadily, clutching his side. His face, which was twisted in pain, was grazed and already showing signs of a bruise.

'Tricks,' said Standish to Roberts.

She nodded glumly. 'Tricks.'

Standish turned to face Harris and his quarry. 'Nothing changes, eh, Jack? I mean, absolutely nothing changes, does it?'

'I don't know what you mean,' replied the inspector, letting one of the uniforms take Michaels. Harris noticed Forrest being loaded into a van. 'Right, Jamie lad, that's the both of them so let's talk protocol.'

'Protocol, Jack?' Standish could contain himself no longer. 'Protocol? Protocol around here means that we do not beat up—'

'Oh, give over, Jamie. He had it coming, you know that. Besides, he went for me. I was just acting in self-defence.' Ignoring the DI's darkening expression, he added, 'Now then, it seems to me that my murder trumps your robbery so I would like to take them back to Levton Bridge tonight. Can you arrange that? Not sure it's a good idea to take them back ourselves.'

'Maybe murder does trump robbery but they are not leaving Manchester tonight. If you want to interview them, you will have to do it here.'

Harris again looked for a moment as if he was about to argue with the detective inspector but thought better of it, held up his hands and started walking towards the Land Rover.

'Have it your way,' he said.

When the inspector was out of earshot, Jamie Standish looked at Roberts.

'He does know that he's in my patch, doesn't he?' he asked with a hint of disbelief in his voice. 'I mean, he does know, doesn't he?'

'Maybe he does, Jamie,' said Roberts, following the inspector. 'Maybe he doesn't. You never can tell with Jack Harris.'

Once the two detectives were back in the Land Rover, Roberts glanced at the inspector.

'You do push it too far sometimes,' she said quietly.

'Yeah, I know.' He did not sound contrite.

'I thought Standish was acting a bit funny when he came out to meet us. Now I know why.'

'Jamie isn't pissed off because I slap the odd suspect around,' said Harris. 'No, Jamie Standish is pissed off because I slept with his wife.'

Back in Levton Bridge, the police van was cruising through the market place for the fifth time that night when something caught the driver's attention. He drove slowly over the cobbles to the war memorial, bringing the vehicle to a halt and winding down the window to allow himself a better look.

'Damn,' he murmured.

'What you seen?' asked his colleague, leaning over. 'Ah. That isn't good.'

'Too right it isn't good,' said the driver as the two officers got out and walked up to the memorial. 'There'll be hell to pay for this. Harris will go off on one, that's for sure.'

For a few moments, the officers looked gloomily at the letters 'DIS' scrawled in red paint across the names of the area's war dead. The paint was still glistening.

'This has only just been done,' said the driver, turning round quickly. 'Whoever did it can't have gone far.'

But the market place was deserted.

CHAPTER EIGHTEEN

'Jamie, there's something else we want to do after we've interviewed Forrest and Michaels,' said Harris as the Levton Bridge detectives sat in the DI's office, cradling mugs of tea. 'Maybe in the morning before we head back.'

'What is it?' Standish seemed guarded.

'We want to visit a place in Sale Street. Sells military memorabilia.'

'Not sure why you would be interested in that. It's been there for years, Jack. It's completely kosher. Surely it's not linked to your murder inquiry?'

'It cropped up during some inquiries my sergeant was doing.'

'Well, he's wasting your time. I bought a couple of things there last year. Couple of cap badges for a project my eldest was doing at school. They're good lads run that, Jack. There's no way they would be mixed up with anyone like Forrest and Michaels.'

'Maybe so,' said Harris, standing up and draining his mug, 'but we would still like to take a look. If nothing else, it will tie up a loose end.'

Standish was about to reply when a man in a dark suit walked into the room, a broad grin on his face.

'They told me Jack Harris was in town,' he said delightedly.

Harris stood up. 'Dennis,' he said as the two men shook

hands. 'Good to see you. Gillian, this is Dennis Maddison, a DCI down here—'

'Detective super now, old son,' said Maddison, pulling up a chair and sitting down. He glanced at Roberts. 'By, we had some times together, me and your governor. Must be five years since I last saw you, Hawk. How you been doing? Not sick of all those sheep yet?'

'Sorry, Dennis.'

'Pity. There's always a place for you here if you change your mind, you know that. Nice result out at the pub. I hope Jamie is affording you all the help you need.'

'Yes, he is, thanks.'

'When you going back to Levton Gate or whatever it's called?'

'In the morning. Jamie's fixed somewhere for us to sleep.'

Maddison's lips twitched but he said nothing. Standish noticed the gesture and frowned.

'Just telling Jamie that we want to drop in on a war memorabilia place out on Sale Street before we go,' said Harris.

'And I was just ...' began Standish.

'Why so interested in it?' asked Maddison.

'Part of our murder inquiry.'

'You need a warrant?'

'There's no way ...' began Standish.

'Please,' said Harris.

'I'll see what I can do,' said Maddison, standing up. 'Listen, when you've interviewed your bad lads, come along to my office, yeah? I've got a nice single malt you'll appreciate. Been waiting for a special occasion – this seems as good as any.'

After the superintendent had walked out into the corridor, Harris also stood up.

'Sale Street tomorrow then,' said the inspector.

'OK,' sighed Standish. 'Have it your way.'

'I usually do,' said Harris, his voice echoing back from the corridor. 'You know that, Jamie.'

Standish glared after him but said nothing. Roberts tried not to smile as she followed the inspector out of the office. As she did so, she glanced back at Standish, who sat at his desk, staring after them. He looked so forlorn, she thought.

Downstairs, the Levton Bridge detectives were about to enter the interview room when the inspector's mobile rang. Gallagher, said the screen.

'Matty lad,' said the inspector, taking the call. 'What you got?'

'It's happened again.'

'What has?'

'Just got a call from control. Someone has vandalized the Levton Bridge war memorial.'

Harris leaned against the wall of the corridor and closed his eyes. Suddenly, he felt very weary; it had been a long day.

'Where the hell was our patrol?' he said after a few moments. 'I told them to watch the bloody thing.'

'Looks like whoever did it must have waited for them to pass.'

'What have they done to it?'

'Same as the other one,' said Gallagher. 'If there was any lingering doubt about it being kids, that has surely gone. It's definitely someone with a message for the world.'

'I take it uniform haven't got anyone for it?'

''Fraid not. They toured the streets but turned up nothing. I got them to check the war memorial at Chapel Hill and there's been nothing further there. Oh, and the one down on the green at Kirkhill, that's OK as well.'

'That's something, I suppose. Where are you?'

'Back in Roxham. Just got home.'

'OK, get uniform to double check something for me, will you...?'

A short while later, Harris joined Gillian Roberts in the

interview room where an anxious Ronny Michaels was sitting at the table. Next to him was the duty solicitor, a sallow, grey-haired man who Harris vaguely recognized from his time in Manchester. Just could not place him. It was often like that when he went back to his old patch. There were only two or three regular attending solicitors in Levton Bridge but in Greater Manchester there were dozens of lawyers and Jack Harris frowned as he surveyed this one; the inspector did not like surprises and the man did not look at all pleased to see him.

'DCI Harris,' said the solicitor in a voice that confirmed the inspector's suspicion. 'We meet again. I had rather hoped that we would not.'

'I didn't know we even had,' murmured Harris. 'Forgive me for being rude but who are you?'

'Lewis,' said the solicitor irritably. 'Arthur Lewis of Lewis, Foreman and Battersley. I represent Mr Michaels in this matter and my client alleges that you assaulted him when he was being arrested.'

'Really?' Harris tried to look surprised. 'I find that difficult to believe.'

'Oh, come on, Inspector, everyone knows your reputation. Surely you recall the last time we met.'

Harris looked at him again and the memory unearthed itself from the back of his mind. He decided to play stupid.

'I am afraid not, Mr Lewis,' he said. 'You will have to enlighten me. Did I arrest you for something? Not embezzling funds, were we?'

'Gerry Hacking,' said the lawyer angrily. 'Another person whom you assaulted during an arrest.'

'There's a pattern emerging here,' said Harris, giving the merest of winks to Roberts, who sat there, not quite sure what to make of the confrontation.

'I am happy that we agree on the point,' said Lewis.

'Not sure what point we agree on, Mr Lewis. I was

thinking that you should not be so quick to represent clients with overactive imaginations.'

'Perhaps they are more tolerant of your methods in the backwater where you work these days but down here we do not stand for—'

'If your client wants to submit a formal complaint, I suggest he does it when we are finished here,' said Harris, tiring of the game. 'For the moment, your talents might be more gainfully employed on more pressing matters. Your client is in trouble up to his neck.'

Michaels, who had been enjoying the encounter between detective and solicitor, looked anxious again.

'In which case,' said Lewis, 'perhaps you would like to explain exactly what he is doing here. As far as he is aware, he was having a quiet drink with friends when a large number of police officers burst into the hostelry in question. Next thing he knows, you are launching an unwarranted and unnecessary assault on his person.'

'Did your client tell you that, as he was being arrested, he admitted being complicit in the murder of an elderly man in my area?'

The lawyer glanced at Michaels. 'Is this true?' asked Lewis.

'I might have said something but I never said I killed him. It were Dave done that.'

'But you did nothing to stop the assault?' said Harris with an edge to his voice. 'Did you?'

Michaels shook his head. 'Dave would have killed me as well,' he said.

'So, Mr Lewis,' said Harris sweetly, 'how would you like to proceed?'

The lawyer looked at the inspector with a glum expression on his face but did not reply. Everyone in the room knew that he had been outmanoeuvred. Gillian Roberts allowed herself a slight smile; whatever you might think of the inspector's methods, she thought, there was no denying that he achieved results. Roberts had always struggled with the questions raised by Jack Harris's occasional lapses. She knew it was wrong, of course she did, but there were times, if she was honest with herself, when such methods were justified. And the graze on Ronny Michaels' cheek paled into obscene insignificance when compared to the terrible injuries sustained by Harold Leach. Maybe the ends did justify the means. She would never voice such thoughts aloud, and definitely not in the presence of Curtis, but sometimes … just sometimes … As so often in such situations she found herself coming down on the side of Jack Harris and, without realizing she had done it, the DI gave a little nod.

'So, Ronny,' said Harris, 'from what you've said so far, am I to understand that you were in Harold Leach's cottage last night?'

'Will I be kept out of this if I tell you everything?' asked Michaels hopefully.

'I am not sure the inspector can make those kind of decisions,' said the lawyer. 'My advice would be to keep quiet and see if—'

'It might mean we could put in a good word for you,' interrupted Harris, ignoring the solicitor's glare. 'If you didn't actually kill Harold, the CPS might consider a conspiracy charge rather than murder itself. But I can't make any promises. The CPS might just as easily regard you both as equally responsible.'

Michaels glanced at his lawyer. 'Is he right?' he asked. 'Might it do me some good if I tell him what I know?'

'I suppose it might,' said Lewis grudgingly. 'But, like he says, there is no guarantee of it.'

'What will happen if I don't tell him?'

'I imagine that Mr Harris would have no alternative than to see you charged with murder.' The lawyer sounded reluctant as he made the comment.

'I'll tell you what happened then but I never hurt him, Mr Harris, you have to believe me. It were all down to Dave Forrest.'

'So what happened? You got there in the early hours of the morning, I think?'

'Yeah. Dave forced the back door then we searched the living room. Dave suggested we wake the old man because we couldn't find the medal. I didn't want to do it but Dave said it was the only way.'

'I assume Harold refused to tell you where it was?'

'He was a tough old bird. Kept saying we had no right to take it. He tried to punch Dave. That was when it kicked off. Dave, he was furious. Just kept hitting him. Kept demanding to know where the medal was but the old feller, he wouldn't tell him.' Michaels closed his eyes for a few moments and when he opened them again the detectives could see that they were glistening with tears. 'It were awful, Mr Harris. Dave just kept hitting him. If only he'd told us where the thing was, Dave would have stopped. I kept telling Dave to stop hurting him. You know I don't like violence. Mr Harris.'

'There's a lorry driver with early onset Alzheimer's would like to disagree with you.'

'I never attacked him either. I told you that at the time.'

'You'll be nominated for the Nobel Peace Prize next,' said Harris sardonically. 'Besides, the jury disagreed. Now here we are in a similar situation. You're either lying through your teeth or you're a remarkably unlucky man. What do you reckon, Inspector?' Harris glanced at Roberts.

'Certainly stretches the imagination,' she said. 'Was Harold dead when you left the cottage?'

'Dave said he were just knocked out.'

'And you believed him?' asked Roberts.

'Don't answer that question,' said the solicitor quickly.

Michaels looked down at the desk again and said nothing.

'Not sure he has to,' said Harris. 'Tell me, Ronny. The

downstairs was a wreck. That was down to you as well, I assume?'

'We couldn't find the medal in his bedroom so we searched the living room again. Dave went berserk, ripping drawers out. I was frightened that someone would hear and kept telling him that we had to get out of there.'

'But you found it in the end?'

'He'd hidden it in the lining of one of the chairs. We couldn't get out of there fast enough.'

'Was there just the two of you?' asked Harris.

'Yeah.'

'Does the name Lenny Portland mean anything to you?'

'Never heard of him. Should I of?'

'What about Barry Gough?'

Michaels shook his head. 'No idea who he is either,' he said.

'Or a bloke called Rob Mackey?'

'What is this? You better not be trying to pin anything else on me. I don't know none of them.'

'We think someone from our area tipped you off about Harold's VC. Officers down here have told us that they reckon you have an associate from our area. He was seen getting the train to Roxham.'

'Yeah, that's where he lives but it weren't any of them blokes you mentioned. It was some bloke that Dave knows from when they were in prison together.'

'He got a name?'

'Danny. Danny Marks, I think it was. I only met him a couple of times. Once when he asked us to do the job, the other one when he took the medal off us.'

'I know Danny Marks from when I worked in Roxham,' said Roberts, glancing at Harris. 'He's a fence. Sell his own grandmother if he could get the right price. So, stealing the VC was his idea, Ronny?'

'Yeah. Said he had met this American in Roxham in a pub.

They get talking and this American, he's over on business or something, says he can get a good price for medals back home. Got right excited when Danny said he might be able to get a VC for him.'

'This American got a name?' asked Harris.

'Nah. And whoever he was, he's gone home now. Flew out tonight. That's why we had to do the job last night.'

'And you're sure that none of the names I mentioned were involved? If you're lying to protect—'

'Why would I protect them?' protested Michaels. 'I've just dropped Dave Forrest and Danny Marks in the shit, and that Yank fellow as well. Why would I lie about the others?'

'He's got a point,' said Roberts.

Harris nodded bleakly. 'I suppose,' he said, standing up.

'Can I go now?' asked Michaels. 'You said you'd put a word in for me....'

'Oh, come on, Ronny,' said Harris as he headed for the door, followed by Roberts. 'Like I said, you're in this up to your neck. Do you really think that the CPS will go easy on you?'

'Hang on a minute,' said the lawyer. 'You said that you would....'

'Besides,' said Harris, opening the door to reveal a stern-faced Jamie Standish standing in the corridor, 'even if we did go easy on you, I think the DI here wants a chat. Old fellow got himself duffed up and all for the sake of a medal. Sound familiar, Ronny?'

Michaels gave his lawyer an anxious look as Standish took a seat at the table.

'This could be a long night, Ronny,' said Standish with a thin smile. 'A very long night indeed, son.'

Once out in the corridor, Gillian Roberts patted the DCI on the shoulder.

'Well done, guv,' she said. 'Well done indeed. Even if Forrest says nothing, forensics should be able to tie them to the job. And Michaels' testimony would play well with a jury, wouldn't it?'

'I guess. Come on, let's see if two hard-working detectives can get a bacon sandwich at this time of night.'

'Good idea, I'm famished,' said Roberts as they walked along the dimly lit corridor. 'What about this American guy? What we going to do about him?'

'Not sure what we can do,' said Harris, glancing at his watch. 'Last time I was at Manchester, there were loads of flights for America. Our man could be on any one of them. Assuming he's flying from Manchester, that is. Without a name we've got little chance. We'll just have to hope that Customs clock the medal.'

Ten minutes later, the officers were seated at a table by the canteen window, sipping from mugs of tea as they stared down at the empty night-time street and awaited the delivery of their food. Harris's mobile phone rang.

'No peace for the wicked,' he sighed.

'And sometimes you can be very wicked indeed.'

Harris smiled and took the call. 'Matty lad. Uniform do what I said? Am I right?'

'Yeah, you are. George Mackey's name is obscured by the painted letters. There's a few others, mind.'

'Nevertheless, first thing in the morning, I want Esther Morritt lifting. I can't risk this going any further with Remembrance Sunday so close.'

'Will do. You getting anywhere?'

'Got them both. Caught Michaels down a back alley. He couldn't wait to spill his guts.'

'You didn't help him, by any chance?'

'I don't know what you mean, Matty lad.' The inspector glanced at Roberts. 'Everyone seems to think that I'm not to be trusted. Believe me, I played it by the book.'

'Which one, though?' said the sergeant. He did not wait for a reply. 'What about the others? Portland et al? Michaels implicate any of them?'

'Says he has never heard of them.'

'You believe him?'

'I am afraid I do.' Harris looked at Roberts, who nodded.

'Which leaves us with Forrest and Michaels.'

'Yeah, and a guy from Roxham. We need to pick him up. Did you track down the traffic officer who stopped Forrest's car in Levton Bridge?'

'Yeah, he was on leave, fishing somewhere in the Lake District, but we found him and showed him the mug shots. Says he is pretty sure the driver was Forrest.'

The inspector looked up as the canteen woman brought over their sandwiches.

'Thanks, pet,' he said.

'You've never called me pet before,' said Gallagher.

Harris chuckled.

'So when you back?' asked Gallagher.

'Tomorrow. Jamie Standish is sorting out an overnight stay for us. I was going to suggest we bunk down round his place but for some reason he declined.'

'Am I missing something?' asked Gallagher as he heard Roberts roar with laughter in the background.

'No, but I might be,' said Harris, grinning.

The two detectives had just finished their sandwiches when a plain-clothes officer walked over to the table.

'Forrest is ready,' he said.

As the final light went out in Laurel House, plunging the building into darkness, a figure emerged from the bushes at the bottom of the garden. Having stood and listened to the silence of the night for a few moments, he started walking across the lawn.

CHAPTER NINETEEN

'You manage to check Forrest's car?' asked Harris as the Levton Bridge detectives followed the officer out of the canteen, along the corridor and down the stairs.

'He'd tried to hide it in his garage. It's blue now, mind. It's had a re-spray but we reckon it's the same one your lot stopped. Our traffic guy reckons it's got a new rear bulb.'

'Excellent. Did the plates match with the one we stopped?'

'No, but that doesn't account for much round here. This lot swap plates all the time.' As they reached the door of the interview room, the detective turned to look at them. 'Don't tell my gaffer I said this – he's a bit of an old lady, is Jamie – but if it's true you battered Ronny Michaels, there won't be many round here complaining. They were pretty angry about what he did to that old feller over on Kelley Road. Michaels had it coming, if you ask me.'

'Thank you,' said Harris, pushing his way into the interview room.

He and Roberts took their seats across the desk from a glowering Dave Forrest. Sitting next to him was another lawyer. Harris recognized him from days of old as well.

'Mr Lucas,' said the inspector affably. 'How nice to meet you again.'

'I am not sure I can say the same about yourself,' said Lucas coldly. 'At least you did not beat up my client so that's something to be grateful for, I suppose. What do you want to talk to him about, Mr Harris? Your colleague mentioned something about an incident in Levton Bridge but my client does not even know where it is. From my understanding, it's a rural backwater, is it not?'

'That's two of you have used that phrase tonight,' said Harris. He stared at Forrest. 'Sure you don't know where it is, Dave?'

'Never heard of it.' Forrest seemed brash. Confident.

'I suppose that means you have never heard of a little village called Chapel Hill either, then?'

'S'right.'

'Funny that,' said Harris, glancing at Roberts. 'Is it not, Inspector?'

'Very funny.'

'Perhaps you would like to desist from these silly little games and tell my client why he is being questioned?' said the lawyer icily.

'He is being held in connection with the death of an elderly war veteran called Harold Leach,' explained Harris. 'Mr Leach's body was found in his home yesterday and we believe your client was the one who killed him. We believe that he and Ronny Michaels were robbing the place. We believe they were after Mr Leach's VC, which they sold through an intermediary to an American businessman.'

'Rubbish!' snorted Forrest. 'I told you, I ain't never been to this Chapel Hill place and, what's more, I don't know any Americans.'

'See you've had the car fixed,' said Harris blandly.

Consternation flickered across Forrest's face but only for a second.

'What do you mean?' he asked, quickly regaining his composure. 'I ain't got a—'

'You were stopped in Levton Bridge by one of our traffic officers. Your back light was out. He recognized you from your picture.'

'That all you got?' said Forrest dismissively. 'Some plod checking lights reckons he's seen me in a place I've never even been to?'

'I must admit,' said the lawyer, clipping closed his briefcase and standing up, 'that it all sounds rather flimsy. If that really is all you've got, Mr Harris, we are leaving now.'

'Yeah,' said Forrest, also standing up. 'We're—'

'Fair enough,' said Harris, as they headed for the door. 'Oh, before you do go, Ronny Michaels seems to think that you killed the old man. Now where would he have got such a crazy idea from, Dave?'

Forrest turned to stare at the detective.

'He wouldn't,' he said; all the colour had drained from his face.

'Funny how you think you know someone, isn't it, David?'

Twenty-five minutes later, the officers emerged into the corridor and Harris leaned wearily against a wall.

'Banged to rights,' said Roberts, her eyes gleaming. 'Banged to bloody rights the two of them. Jesus, we're on a roll!'

'I guess.'

'What do you mean, you guess? The lawyer clearly thought so, trying to get his client to suggest it was an accident. No jury in the land will go for manslaughter, though. Not a hope in hell.'

'I imagine not.'

'I don't get it,' said Roberts. 'You don't seem excited by any of this. Think how pleased everyone will be. Think how pleased Curtis will be. You've solved a high-profile murder and got enough on Lenny Portland to at least warrant charges of—'

'I can't help feeling that we are missing something.'

'Like what?'

'Well, if I knew that, Gillian.' Harris frowned. 'There's something else happening here. Someone is trying to send out a message with those attacks on the war memorials but we're not reading it properly. And if there's one thing I don't like, Gillian, it's surprises. I do not like them at all.'

'I remember your birthday party,' said Roberts, nodding.

CHAPTER TWENTY

The first grey light of day was streaking the sky when Matty Gallagher and half a dozen uniformed officers walked up the Roxham street, halting halfway up at a terraced house with a red door. Gallagher knocked loudly, the noise deadened by the mist that was hanging over the town.

'Police!' he shouted.

No answer. Gallagher nodded to one of the uniformed officers who walked forwards with his hydraulic ram and smashed his way through the door. Gallagher and the officers ran inside and the sergeant thundered up the stairs and burst into the bedroom, where a man was struggling out of bed.

'Danny Marks,' said Gallagher. 'I am arresting you on suspicion of conspiracy to murder.'

Jack Harris sat in the hotel restaurant and picked moodily at his cooked breakfast. Sitting opposite him, Gillian Roberts sipped her tea.

'Not exactly a ray of sunshine, are we?' she said. 'Not still worrying about the war memorial thing?'

'Sorry.' Harris gave her a faint smile. 'Just can't get it out of my head.'

'Could be as simple as kids after all. Maybe you are reading too much into it?'

'That's what Roger Barnett reckons.'

'Then I withdraw the comment immediately,' she said, reaching for another slice of toast. 'I imagine he only said it because it stops him actually investigating anything. Gives him more time for chatting up the pretty young things in the typing pool.'

'That's what I said. Then there's Mackey. Given that he's not tied up with the murder, why is he running away?' The inspector's mobile rang and he took it out of his jacket pocket. 'Perhaps this is our answer, eh?'

'We can only hope. Sick of staring at your gloomy face.'

'I thank you for those few kind words,' murmured the inspector, lifting the phone to his ear. 'DCI Harris, who is this?'

'Good morning, sir,' said a young man's voice. 'This is DC Stafford from the fraud squad at Roxham. They said you were in Manchester. Can you talk?'

'Sure.'

'I understand you are trying to track down a chap called Rob Mackey?'

'We are, though not sure why. We've got nothing on him. Why you after him?'

'We received an email from our counterparts in Los Angeles, who were called in by a large firm of antique dealers in the city. A recent audit revealed discrepancies in the company's accounts and further inquiries pointed to bogus invoices from Rob Mackey, who is their representative in the UK.'

'Really?' Harris sat forward. 'Now that is interesting.'

'More than interesting. Their checks uncovered invoices stretching back the best part of ten years and worth 1.4 million dollars. All for items that appear not to have existed.'

'Did the Americans pay up?'

'Yes.'

'Curtis queries it if I'm a penny out on my mileage. Surely someone knew what was happening?'

'Yes. A guy who worked for the American company. Mackey submitted invoices for goods shipped over from the UK and this fellow waved them through then falsified the records. All very slick until he made a mistake and the auditors clocked it.'

'They get him?'

'The firm say he's been in the UK on business. Comes over here quite often to see Mackey. Seems he flew out of Manchester last night on his way home. Chap called Grover Randall. When they looked into his background, they discovered that he's got form for fraud. Got three names as well. Grover Randall's his latest.'

'I wonder,' murmured Harris.

'Wonder what?'

'I wonder if he's got a VC in his bag. Where do we come into all this?'

'US police will arrest Randall when he touches down – what time is it now? 8.45. They may already have done so. And they want us to pick Mackey up.'

'Wish we could. He disappeared yesterday. I guess he knew what was happening.'

'Almost certainly. The inquiry has been very hush-hush but the firm's payments department have just written to him in error, telling him no further invoices will be honoured. Sounds like your man put two and two together and scarpered.'

'Well, he can't run for ever,' said Harris. 'No man can. And I should know, I've tried.'

A small crowd had gathered round Levton Bridge's war memorial as the sullen light of day revealed the full extent of the vandalism. Standing apart from the other people, Matty Gallagher gloomily surveyed the damage then glanced over to where Roger Barnett was trying to ensure that the growing crowd did not get too close. With a sigh, the sergeant looked back at the memorial, where a forensics officer was crouched, examining the paint.

'Anything we can use?' asked Gallagher, walking over to him.

'Sorry, Matty,' said the officer without looking up, 'it's like the other one. The paint is the type you could get anywhere.'

'You're right, I'm afraid. After Chapel Hill, we checked the local hardware stores and they'd all sold loads of the stuff. I never realized the sodding colour was so popular.'

'Looks like the type my missus used in our downstairs loo.' The forensics officer finally looked up. 'Having a dump in a bright red loo, I tell you, it's not exactly conducive. Especially if you've had jalfrezi the night before. The colour is quite re—'

'Yeah, thanks for sharing that. Very useful.'

'Anything to oblige,' said the forensics officer, grinning. 'I'll try to match a sample with Chapel Hill but even if we do I'm not sure where it gets us.'

'I hate to think what kind of sample you're referring to. God knows we need something, though. All the sales were cash so there's no record. Billy over in Porteous Street did remember selling a pot to the vicar last year. Perhaps I should arrest him.'

'Stop him preaching those criminally long sermons.'

'Quite the wit, aren't we? It's like an audience with Max Miller.'

'Who?' said the forensics officer, scraping at the memorial.

'Never mind. Unfortunately, no one can remember Esther Morritt buying paint.'

'She still your favourite then?' asked the forensics officer, straightening up and stepping back from the memorial.

'She's the only one with a good enough reason to hate Rob Mackey.'

'There's plenty of people with reason to hate Rob Mackey. I don't blame them. He's an arrogant so and so.' The officer noticed Butterfield and James Larch walking across the market place. 'Hey, is it true that he has been dobbing young Alison?'

'How the…?'

'Never mind how, is it true?'

''Fraid so but I wouldn't mention it to her – well, not unless you fancy keeping your testicles in a box.'

'Point taken. Mind, she's better than that, way better than that.' The forensics officer returned his attention to the memorial. 'That's assuming that this is about Rob Mackey, of course. I mean, there's plenty more names on here.'

'We're not getting far with them, though. Apart from Mackey's father, they died at least sixty years ago.' Gallagher leaned forward towards the memorial. 'I mean, this one was killed in 1914. Who the hell could hang on to a grudge that long? Not even Harris could do that.'

'Not so sure, Matty.' The forensics man clicked shut his case. 'I heard your governor bawled out Roger Barnett last night. And they have known each other for twenty-odd years. Anyhoo, can't do much more here. It rained in the early hours so there's very little to go on.'

'OK, thanks, Brian,' said Gallagher, watching him walk across the market place and nod at Butterfield and Larch as he passed them. As the detectives neared him, the sergeant asked: 'Anything?'

'Nothing,' said Butterfield. 'We checked with the pub landlords. None of them heard or saw anything last night.'

'We checked if Portland stayed in the boozer last night,' added Larch. 'The landlord of the Duck reckoned he was kaylied.'

Before the officers could reply, they were approached by a worried-looking Henry Maitlin, who stood and shook his head as he surveyed the vandalized war memorial.

'Terrible, absolutely terrible,' he said. He lowered his voice. 'Listen, keep this under your hats for the moment but we're thinking of calling off tomorrow's ceremony.'

'Harris reckoned you might suggest that,' said Gallagher. 'The governor reckons this town should honour its dead whatever the risks.'

'But it's too big a risk, Matthew. Think of the shame it would bring on Levton Bridge if something happened.'

'Let's not be too hasty.' Gallagher lowered his voice. 'Between you and me, we're going to lift Esther now.'

'About time. That woman has caused more than enough trouble.'

'But what if it's not her?' asked Butterfield when Maitlin had gone. 'What if the dishonour does not relate to the Mackeys at all? And I am not saying that because I was going out with Rob.'

'Was?' said the sergeant.

'Not sure we've got much of a future after all this.'

'You're probably right. Maybe you've got a point about the Mackeys, though. Could be nothing to do with them. If Esther's in the clear, we'll lift Barry Gough, rattle his cage.'

'What about the British Legion?' said Larch, looking across to where Maitlin was deep in conversation with an elderly man. 'Remember what Harris has been banging on about? Those other incidents? What if the Legion is the target?'

'Who on earth would have a grudge against a load of old codgers?' said Gallagher as the officers started walking across the market place. 'We got a secret Nazi cell operating in Levton Bridge?'

Larch shrugged. 'Folks are funny, Sarge.'

'Best get looking then,' said Gallagher, glancing up at the town clock as it struck ten. 'Because by my reckoning we have twenty-five hours to stop the Remembrance ceremony being wrecked. In the meantime, we'll go and nick Esther Morritt.'

'We?' said Butterfield, noticing that the sergeant was looking at her.

'Yeah, you're going with me. I'm not facing the mad old baggage myself and that's final.'

Sitting on the bed in his motel room, Rob Mackey stared at the Ceefax story on the television screen. He had read it three times.

Police in Manchester last night arrested two men in connection with the murder of ninety-three-year-old war veteran Harold Leach, a holder of the Victoria Cross.

Officers from Greater Manchester Police, working with colleagues from the North West Force, arrested the men after a raid on a pub in east Manchester.

The men have been charged with the murder of Mr Leach, from the North Pennines village of Chapel Hill. Detective Chief Inspector Jack Harris, the officer leading the investigation into Mr Leach's death, said both men would appear before magistrates in Levton Bridge later today.

Detective Inspector Jamie Standish, of Greater Manchester Police, said the men had also been charged in connection with a robbery on a ninety-one-year-old man in the city earlier this year.

Rob Mackey picked up his bag and left the room. 'Run, rabbit, run,' he murmured.

CHAPTER TWENTY-ONE

Jack Harris and Gillian Roberts left their hotel and drove the short distance to the Sale Street industrial estate. Pulling the Land Rover up outside a run-down workshop, they saw that Jamie Standish was already waiting.

'He looks cheerful,' said Roberts.

Harris said nothing and the Levton Bridge officers got out of the vehicle and walked up to the building.

'You got it?' said Harris to Standish.

Standish fished in his jacket pocket and produced a document which he handed to the inspector.

'Yeah,' he said. 'Took a bit of hard talking, I can tell you. Frankly, I felt a right dick and if the super hadn't—'

'You got it anyway.' Harris nodded to the door, which bore no sign. 'You want to do the honours? It is in your patch, after all.'

'Nice of you to remember,' murmured Standish. 'And no, I do not want to do the honours. This is a wild-goose chase and when it goes tits up you can handle the flak. Like I keep telling you, our intelligence hasn't turned up anything to suggest that this place is anything other than legit. Surely you are not suggesting that your mate Leckie has missed something?'

'No one's perfect,' said Harris, knocking on the door. He winked at Roberts. 'I have even heard suggestions that I may be a flawed human being. Besides, I've got a feeling about this one.'

'And you don't argue with his instincts,' said Roberts, glancing at Standish. 'Rule number one of working with Jack Harris. You should know that, Jamie.'

'I've had enough of his instincts, thank you.'

Harris gave a slight smile and knocked again, louder this time. After a couple of minutes, the door was opened by a man, whose eyes widened when he saw them.

'Jesus,' he said weakly.

'Morning, Barry,' said Harris cheerfully, walking past Barry Gough before he could protest. 'What a surprise to see you here. How's it going in the world of double standards? This where you make your placards then?'

Gough leaned against the wall and closed his eyes. When he opened them, the officers had already pushed their way through the interior door that led into the dimly lit workshop.

'Hey!' shouted Gough, following them into the room. 'You can't ...'

'Actually we can,' said Harris, holding the warrant up. 'Well, well, what do we have here then?'

The detectives looked at three young men standing by a series of wooden crates and eyeing the officers uneasily.

'What's this then, Barry?' asked Harris, turning round to Gough. 'You getting into the mail order business?'

'It's nothing, Harris. Just ...'

'Just a bit of war memorabilia, I imagine,' said the inspector, walking over to the pile of boxes. His path was barred by one of the other men but a hard look cleared the way. 'And what would I find if I opened one of these then?'

'Nowt much,' mumbled the man, taking a couple of steps backwards.

'Yeah,' said Gough, trying to appear calm but coming over as nervous. 'Cap badges, uniforms, that kind of thing. We're not doing anything wrong. This is all legit.'

'Don't you think it's weird that a man who protests about

the evils of war should also be making money from selling this kind of stuff?' asked Roberts.

'So if I'm guilty of anything it's double standards.' Gough pointed to the door. 'It ain't against the law, lady. Now get out. You ain't got no right ...'

'Your favourite phrase,' said Harris with a thin smile, holding up the document, 'but this is a warrant to search this place. We always like to do things by the book, as you know.'

The comment was not lost on Standish, who frowned but said nothing.

'But we ain't done nothing wrong,' protested one of the men, gesturing to Standish. 'You ask him – he's bought stuff from us. For his boy. For a school project or something.'

Harris glanced at Standish, waiting for a response, but the detective inspector did not say anything, preferring to look away. Harris walked over to a table and picked up a screwdriver before prising open the lid to one of the crates to reveal carefully folded uniforms.

'See,' said Gough, reaching over to close the lid. 'Ain't nothing illegal. Now get out before I—'

''Fraid I can't do that, Barry. I'm a suspicious bugger.' Harris lifted the uniforms out of the crate and produced an army-issue revolver. 'This legal as well?'

Harris gave a smile as he glanced at the amazed Standish, whose eyes seemed magnetically drawn to the weapon. Even Gillian Roberts looked surprised.

'That's one hell of a school project your lad was doing, Jamie,' said Harris.

Barry Gough seemed rooted to the ground but the other three men started to run towards the door, one of them knocking over a startled Standish as they fled. Getting quickly back to his feet, the DI gave chase, followed by Harris. Gough made as if to follow them but found his way blocked by the resolute form of Gillian Roberts.

'Not worth it, Barry,' she said. 'Besides, where would you run? It's a long way back to Levton Bridge.'

For a moment, the detective inspector thought that he was going to strike out at her but, after considering his predicament for a few moments, Gough gave a shrug and held out his hands to be cuffed.

'Not sure there's any need for that, Barry,' said Roberts. 'Just stand there and don't try any funny business.'

Out in the lobby, one of the fleeing men wrenched open the door only to be grabbed by Jack Harris, who whirled him round by his shoulder. The man gave a cry and lashed out with his fist, the blow catching Harris on the side of the face. With a grunt the inspector fell against the wall and all three men burst out into the morning sunshine to be confronted by the sight of several uniformed officers standing and chatting next to a police van. Within moments, and after a brief struggle, two of the men were apprehended. Having seen them marched back into the building, glum looks on their faces, Standish turned to see the man who had struck Harris running away with the inspector closing rapidly on him. Standish cursed and set off after them.

Harris caught up with the man a little further down the road, grabbing at his jacket and sending him sprawling on the tarmac. The man leapt back to his feet and swung another punch at the inspector who, this time, swayed inside it. Standish slowed to a walk as Harris closed in on his quarry.

'Come on, son,' said Harris, holding out a hand. 'This does not make sense. Give it up, eh? We don't want anyone else hurt, do we?'

The man hesitated; he had drawn blood with his punch and both Harris and Standish could see the fear in his eyes. Harris took a step closer. Standish held his breath. The man nodded and allowed Harris to slip on the handcuffs and walk his suspect back towards Standish.

'See,' said Harris, 'you think you know someone.'

Standish gave a rueful smile. 'Guess it's possible to make a mistake,' he said.

'Guess it is,' said Harris. He gave the slightest of nods. 'Me included, Jamie.'

Standish nodded and the three men walked back into the workshop where Harris approached the crates again. Roberts gave Standish a quizzical look as she nodded in the direction of the uniformed officers.

'I thought you said there wasn't any need for back-up?' she said. 'We wouldn't find anything? The warrant was a waste of time? School project blah blah.'

Standish gave her a rueful look. 'Are all Levton Bridge detectives arsey gits?' he asked.

'Pretty much. So, you going to explain the back-up then?'

'Your governor may be infuriating but, like you said, if there is one thing I learned about him when he was down here, it was not to doubt his instincts.'

'Wise words, Jamie,' said Roberts. She looked at what Harris had produced from the crate. 'Oh, will you look at that? It's like Christmas come early.'

Harris had produced several more revolvers. He reached in again and pulled out a machine gun.

'Jesus Christ,' murmured Standish, walking over to the chief inspector. He glanced at Harris. 'Proper little arsenal, isn't it? We looking at calling in the anti-terrorism boys, Jack?'

'Could be.'

'It's nothing like that,' said Gough quickly; he had gone pale. 'Besides, it's deactivated. And it's not new. Dates from 1954.'

'Not sure anyone standing at the wrong end of the barrel would appreciate the distinction,' said Harris. 'Besides, do you know how easy it is to deactivate a gun, Barry?'

Gough looked bleakly at him.

'Thought so,' said Harris.

He prised open the lid of the next crate. Again, he removed some uniforms then brought out a small box, opening the lid and holding it up so that the others could see.

'Medals,' said Roberts. 'Now there's interesting. Where might you have got them from, I wonder, Barry?'

'Not from Harold Leach,' said Gough quickly.

'Then who?' said Harris with an edge to his voice. 'Some other veteran who regarded them as among his most precious possessions?'

Gough gave them a sick look. Harris placed the box down on the nearby table and leaned further into the crate.

'Get out,' he said quietly. He gestured to the others. There was urgency in his voice now. 'Get your people out of here, Jamie. Get everyone out of here.'

'Why, what's…?'

Standish's voice tailed away as the inspector held up a hand grenade.

The smartly dressed businessman had just cleared Customs at Los Angeles Airport when the two plain-clothes police officers approached him.

'Grover Randall?' said one of them.

'Yes.'

'Come with me, please, sir.'

They took him into an airless room where they began to search his bags.

'They have already been checked,' said Randall.

'We are aware of that, sir,' said the officer and continued searching, eventually holding up a small paper package, watched by a perspiring Randall. 'And what might this be?'

'A present for my wife,' said Randall but it didn't sound convincing.

'She like war memorabilia, does she?' said the officer, unwrapping the package and holding up a Victoria Cross.

*

Gallagher and Butterfield were driving past the front door of Laurel House when they saw a woman standing on the roadside and frantically waving her arms.

'That's Liz Mackey,' said Gallagher, bringing the vehicle to a halt. 'Wonder what's happened now?'

'I'll stay in the car.'

'She doesn't know it's you been dobbing her husband.'

She shot him a beseeching look. 'Please, Matty, let me stay in the car.'

Gallagher nodded. 'This time. And this time only,' he said as he got out of the car. 'Liz, what's the problem? You heard from Rob?'

'Forget that bastard,' she said angrily. 'Follow me, I'll show you.'

Butterfield watched as they disappeared down the tree-lined drive. The constable already knew that there were rumours in the police station that she was the other woman in Rob Mackey's life. She had seen the looks, heard the whispering in corridors. Butterfield knew that it was only a matter of time before the news made its way beyond the police-station walls. The valley had never kept secrets. Things always leaked out. Sometimes, she thought as she sat there, there was a great appeal to the idea of working in the city. A place where no one knew your name and your secrets remained secrets because no one cared. As she waited for Gallagher to return, Butterfield sighed and wished that no one cared about her.

At the end of the drive, the sergeant stood and stared at the letters 'DIS' scrawled across the memorial plaque on the wall of the house.

'Brilliant,' he murmured.

'This is her doing!' exclaimed Liz.

'Whose doing? Who do you think did this, Liz?'

'Who? You know damn well who.'

'Enlighten me.' Gallagher held his breath and thought of Butterfield sitting alone in the car back on the main road.

'That crazy Morritt woman.'

Gallagher breathed a sigh of relief. 'Ah, her,' he said.

'Yes, her. Rob was right. She won't leave us alone. First the memorial in Chapel Hill, now this. And I heard that the memorial in the market square was vandalized last night. I take it you know that George's name is on that as well?'

'We do, yes.' Gallagher walked up to examine the paint. It was still tacky. 'You didn't see anything last night then?'

'Don't you think I would have done something if I had?'

'Did you not even hear anything?'

Hesitation.

'Liz?' he said, looking closely at her. 'Did you hear anything?'

'I didn't hear much last night, Sergeant.' She looked embarrassed. 'I am afraid I had rather too much to drink.'

Gallagher glanced across to the front door to see Bethany emerge.

'She was absolutely plastered,' said the teenager, nodding. 'Whisky. Celebrating my father's decision to run from his responsibilities as usual. Are you going to talk to that Morritt woman?'

'We'll talk to her, Bethany. Don't worry about that.'

'My grandfather deserves better than this,' said the teenager, looking at the vandalized plaque. 'I mean, after what he did for his country.'

'He does, yes. I guess you never met him?'

'Do I look thirty?' she said waspishly. 'And just because I never knew him, it doesn't mean I'm not proud of him.'

'I didn't mean to ...'

'We should remember our fallen war heroes, Sergeant. That was just about the only thing I agreed with my father about. They may be gone but they're still alive in people's hearts, aren't they? I mean they never die, do they?'

'No, they don't,' said the sergeant thoughtfully. He started to walk down the drive. 'We'll keep you informed of developments.'

When he got back to the car, Butterfield looked at him.

'Well?' she said anxiously. 'What happened?'

'Out of the mouths of babes,' he said, easing himself into the driver's seat.

'What?'

'I think we have been looking at the wrong Mackey. I don't think this is about Rob, I think this is about George.'

'But he's been dead thirty years!'

'If you ask me,' said Gallagher, starting the engine, 'he's very much alive to someone.'

The man stumbled in the darkness and pitched forward. He did not feel what had hit him; at first he did not even know that he had been hit. Mind reeling, confused images swirling before his eyes, he sunk to his knees. He slowly turned his head, trying desperately to focus on the spinning world around him, trying to make sense of what had happened. Vision blurred, body now racked with jagged pain, he tried to stand up but his legs buckled and he staggered forward once more, this time to lie still and silent on the cold ground. Looking up, he saw a face staring down at him and heard a voice echoing as if from afar. The voice fell silent and the face receded into the distance as the darkness closed in. The man was alone and he felt cold. He knew in that moment that he was dying. After that, he saw nothing, heard nothing, felt nothing. His was to sleep for ever. It was down to others to honour his memory.

CHAPTER TWENTY-TWO

Shortly before eleven, Harris and Roberts were sitting in the Land Rover and watching the arrival of the bomb disposal team. The building had been sealed off by uniformed officers, who had created a taped cordon to keep back the excited crowd, local people having gathered as word spread about the discovery of the arms cache. Also there were television crews and other reporters.

'Quite a circus,' said Harris, glancing into the back seat where Barry Gough was sitting next to Standish. 'What on earth were you thinking?'

'It seemed a good idea at the time,' said Gough gloomily. 'Besides, I needed the money.'

'I assume the war protesting was a cover?'

'Not as such, no. I went on a couple of protest marches when I was a student.'

'Yet you ended up in the army.'

'Only because there were no jobs. Definitely not because I believed in what they were doing. And before you say it, what we do here does not glorify war. Look, I know you were a soldier, Harris, but even you must realize that what we are doing in Afghanistan is absolutely appalling and it is absolutely correct that we—'

'Skip the party political, son. Besides, your beliefs did not exactly stop you trafficking in arms, did they? Quite a remarkable thing for a man of peace.'

'There's plenty of men of peace have done things which are not compatible with their beliefs.'

'Quite the philosopher, aren't we?'

'Besides, you make it sound worse than it is.'

'How much worse can it be?' asked the inspector, watching the bomb disposal team at work. 'They reckon you've got eleven grenades and half a dozen mortars. All of which could have gone off at any time. Where the hell does it come from, Barry?'

'Most of it's old army issue. Lots of guys have this kind of stuff lying about.'

'Revolvers, maybe, but machine guns? Mortars? And some of the stuff I saw was modern. Where did that come from?'

Gough hesitated.

'You can tell us or wait for the MPs to arrive,' said Harris. 'Not sure they'll be as nice as us, mind.'

Roberts gave Gough a look. 'He's right,' she said. 'They're not all as easy-going as the governor.'

Gough recalled his earlier encounters with the DCI and nodded.

'OK,' he said. 'The modern stuff comes from a couple of lads I knew in the army. They're still in – one of them's a quartermaster – and they smuggle stuff out to us and we sell it on. They get a cut.'

'Where do you sell it on to?' asked Standish.

'Not to criminals if that's what you are thinking. It's just collectors.'

'What's the betting some of your stuff has turned up in the wrong hands?' said Harris. 'You had any armed stuff lately, Jamie?'

'Couple of post office jobs. Least one of them by a guy carrying a revolver. If any of your gear is linked to them, you're for the high jump, sunshine. Deactivated or not, they're still guns.'

Gough looked worried.

'The rest of your stuff,' said Harris, 'the medals and the like. Any of that come from our patch?'

'Maybe.' Guarded now.

'No maybes, Barry,' said Harris. 'You're in this up to your neck – not sure you can make it any worse. Who passes stuff on from our patch?'

'No one.'

'We'll find out whether you tell us or not. We've been watching you. And yes, I know it goes against your human rights. Where does Lenny fit in with this?'

'OK, OK,' sighed Gough. 'He gets hold of some stuff for me. The odd medal. A bayonet once.'

'Stolen?'

'Maybe.'

'Maybe yes. And Philip Morritt? Did he get you some gear?'

'A bit. Couple of medals.'

'His mum reckons he was working with Rob Mackey.'

'She'd say anything to drop him in it,' said Gough with a low laugh. 'Nah, Rob Mackey is nowt to do with us. The man's an arrogant bastard. Do you really think we would have anything to do with him?'

'But Lenny told us that Mackey was involved.'

'You believe everything he tells you? If Lenny told me it was raining I'd stick my head out of the window to see if I got wet. He panicked, said the first thing that came into his mind. And before you say it, he had nowt to do with the death of that old feller either. None of us did.'

'But he was after the medal, wasn't he?'

'I never ask him where the stuff comes from.' Gough noticed the officers' sceptical expressions. 'Honest.'

'I very much doubt that you would even know the meaning of the word, son.' Harris noticed a large car pulling into the road. 'Ah, here's your ride. They're going to love you. Absolutely love you.'

'You said you'd keep them out of it,' protested Gough as he saw the military police officers getting out of the vehicle.

'Not sure I said that, Barry. I reckon this is a military matter when all's said and done. Besides, when they're finished, Anti-Terrorist want a word but only if they can persuade Special Branch to let them go first. They'll be pulling rank like there's no tomorrow.'

'Yeah, you're Mr Popular,' nodded Standish. 'Loads of people want to talk to you, sunbeam.'

'You'll be Levton Bridge's biggest celebrity,' said Harris. 'Hey, if you play your cards right, they'll have you opening the carnival next summer. Assuming you're not inside, mind.'

'What if I gave you something else?' said Gough quickly.

'Like what?'

'Like telling you who is doing them memorials?'

Harris glanced over at the military policemen, who had sought directions from a uniformed constable and were now approaching the Land Rover.

'Start talking, Barry,' said Harris, 'and if I were you, son, I'd do it quickly.'

As Rob Mackey plugged his mobile into the Range Rover's connection point, the phone rang. He glanced down at the screen. Liz. Mackey scowled, switched the phone off, turned on the ignition key and drove out of the motel car park onto the motorway slip road. He did not notice the patrol car parked in the nearby petrol station.

Matty Gallagher hesitated for a moment or two as he and Butterfield stood outside the cottage in Chapel Hill.

'You ready?' he said.

'Not sure I am ever ready for an encounter with Esther Morritt, Sarge. Give me Liz Mackey any day.'

'I know what you mean,' said Gallagher and knocked loudly on the cottage door. 'Oh, well, heydy-ho.'

The door was opened by Esther Morritt.

'Sergeant Gallagher,' she said without warmth in her voice. 'What can I do for you?'

'I am afraid I am going to have to ask you to accompany us to the police station, Esther.'

'Why?' She showed no sign of moving off the doorstep.

'The Levton Bridge war memorial was vandalized last night.'

'I had nothing to do with that. I was here all night.'

'Anyone stand witness to that? Got an exotic love life we know nothing about?'

She glared at him. 'There has been no one since my Arthur died. I am a widow and you well know that, Sergeant.'

'Could be a merry one, though.'

'How dare—'

'Look, can we come in, Esther?' said Gallagher, glancing down the street and noticing curtains twitching in windows. 'I do not really want to talk about this on the doorstep.'

'I'd rather you didn't talk about it at—'

'Have it your way then,' said Gallagher irritably, reaching out to take her by the arm. 'Esther Morritt, I am arr—'

His mobile phone rang.

'Sorry about this,' he said, letting go of her, fishing the device out of his jacket pocket and walking a few yards down the street. After an intense conversation, he returned to the cottage, a sheepish look on his face.

'It would seem,' he said, 'that we owe you an apology. It was wrong of us to try to arrest you. Enjoy the rest of the day. Sorry to have inconvenienced you.'

As the detectives walked down the hill, it struck the sergeant that he would probably never forget the look of triumph on her face.

'What the hell was that about?' asked Butterfield when they were out of her earshot. 'Who was that on the phone?'

'Harris,' said Gallagher gloomily. 'It would appear that

dearest Esther is not public enemy number one after all. Nowhere near, in fact. Well, not unless she's got a stash of machine guns in the outside lavvy.'

The Range Rover was only a couple of miles down the southbound motorway when Rob Mackey saw the flashing blue lights in his rear-view mirror. For a moment he wondered whether to hit the gas, try to outrun them. But run where? he asked himself. Where on earth could he go? Wherever he went, he knew that Jack Harris would always come for him. Mackey recalled Roger Barnett's words back on the green. He'll love arresting you. Absolutely love it. And now Harris had a reason to do it. That letter about the invoices suggested the Americans had become suspicious and there was no way they would not have called in the police. Not with 1.4 mil at stake. Perhaps they knew that Randall Glover had been to see him during his recent visit to the UK. Perhaps they had already arrested him. Perhaps they had found the VC. Thought that Mackey was involved in that as well. Whatever had happened, Mackey was sure that Glover would sing like the proverbial. He'd never trusted the man.

Mackey slowed the vehicle down to a halt on the hard shoulder and waited for the traffic officers to arrest him. At least that would deprive Jack Harris of the pleasure, he thought. A minor victory but it felt like a victory all the same.

Back in Levton Bridge, Philip Curtis was doing his paperwork when there came a knock on his office door.

'Come in,' said the commander, glancing up.

Roger Barnett walked into the room.

'Good morning, Roger,' said Curtis, gesturing to the vacant chair on the other side of the desk. 'What can I do for you?'

'This is a somewhat delicate matter, sir,' said Barnett, sitting down.

'I hope you feel that you can talk to me in confidence.'

'Thank you, sir.' Barnett leaned forward. 'I think you and I may be in the position to make a deal.'

'A deal?' said Curtis, raising an eyebrow. 'I hardly think it is appropriate for district commanders to enter into "deals" with sergeants.'

'Look, sir, I know that you would love an opportunity to get rid of Jack Harris. Well, I wish to make a complaint about his highly unprofessional conduct towards me, which if you play your cards right—'

'Play my cards right?'

'Yes, this will give you a golden opportunity to—'

'Let me stop you there,' said Curtis, putting his pen down on its blotter and leaning back in his seat. 'You are right, Roger, I struggle with Jack Harris. Yes, there are times when he oversteps the mark and yes, there are times when I would like nothing more than for him to retire to that cottage of his and take his blessed dogs with him, especially as they are currently cluttering up my control room. But at the end of the day, he's ten times the police officer you are. The events of the past two days have made that abundantly clear, I would have thought.'

Barnett looked at him in amazement.

'However,' continued Curtis, with a slight smile, 'I do acknowledge your candour in this matter. I like an officer who can communicate concisely and clearly.'

Barnett looked at him suspiciously. 'Sir?'

'Oh, and while I remember,' said Curtis, picking up a piece of paper from his desk, 'headquarters have been on. Would you like a posting back to headquarters, Roger?'

'Very much so, sir,' said Barnett, adding quickly, 'depending on what it is, of course.'

'Oh, you'll love this one. They're setting up a new road safety unit, going round the schools, talking to the kids, that kind of thing. They wondered if we had anyone spare and I immediately thought of you. Right up your street. As it were.'

'Now hang on, sir ...'

'Apparently you will be working with Sergeant Squirrel.'

'What?'

'Sergeant Squirrel. It's their new mascot. They've seconded some young girl from the typing pool to dress up in the costume. I know you take a keen interest in girls from the typing pool, Roger. Apparently, their first campaign is aimed at kids getting off school buses and from what I hear you are also excellent with buses. So, do you accept? Yes? Good. You can start Monday. Close the door on your way out, will you?'

A stunned Roger Barnett walked out of the office, not quite sure what had just happened to him, and Philip Curtis returned to his paperwork, allowing himself an occasional smile.

In the corridor, Barnett was approached by James Larch.

'You heard the news?' said the detective excitedly. 'Not only have they cracked the Harold Leach murder but they've only gone and busted an arms ring as well! And solved the vandalism of the memorials. Bloody amazing. Absolutely bloody amazing.'

Barnett stared gloomily as the detective walked down the corridor but said nothing. For the first in his life, he could not think of anything to say.

Matty Gallagher emerged from the records room in the basement station, carrying a battered old file. Having spent the best part of an hour and a half there, he was feeling cold so he went to the canteen before returning to the CID squad room. Clutching his cup of tea in one hand and the file in the other, he finally reached the squad room where a number of detectives were waiting.

'Well?' asked Larch eagerly as the sergeant walked in. 'Is Barry Gough telling the truth?'

'Sure is,' said Gallagher, placing the file on the table and blowing away the dust. 'We *have* been looking at the wrong Mackey.'

'Looks pretty thin to me,' said Butterfield, picking up the file and removing a couple of sheets of paper.

'But isn't that the point?' Gallagher took a sip of his tea. 'Looks like they assumed it was open and shut. Not sure anyone did much in the way of investigating.'

Before he could elaborate further, the sergeant's mobile rang and he walked out into the corridor. Several minutes later, he walked back into the room, slipping the device into his jacket pocket.

'What's wrong?' asked Larch, seeing the grim expression on the sergeant's face. 'Who was that on the phone?'

'Harris. Turns out Gough gave our guy a shotgun as a thank you for services rendered. Thought he would use it for rabbits.' Gallagher drained his cup of tea. 'I have this awful feeling he has something else in mind. Come on, we had better sort this out before someone gets hurt.'

The man loped through the misty fields, shotgun in hand, until he reached the dry-stone wall, where he paused to survey the gable end poking out of the nearby trees. He gave a thin smile and started walking again.

'Payback,' he said.

Sitting on the sofas in the living room and sipping at their mid-morning coffee, Liz and Bethany Mackey were not aware that the man had emerged from the bushes at the bottom of the garden and was walking with a steady pace across the lawn towards Laurel House.

'When are they going to let you see Dad?' asked Bethany.

'I am not sure, love. They said they were going to interview him at Levton Bridge this afternoon.'

'Did they say much about what he's done wrong?'

'All Sergeant Gallagher said was that he thought it was

something to do with a fraud. God knows what your father has been up to.'

'Then what?' asked Bethany, taking a sip of coffee. 'Will he come back here?'

'Who knows?'

'Will you let him back?'

'I don't want to.'

'Then don't,' said Bethany. 'Let him go and stay with that floosie of his.'

The blast shattered the window.

CHAPTER TWENTY-THREE

'I bet you are really enjoying this,' said Mackey as he sat, arms crossed, next to his solicitor, staring across the desk at Harris and fraud squad officer Daniel Stafford. 'Been waiting a long time, haven't you?'

'I won't deny that I am deriving a certain degree of pleasure out of this,' said Harris. 'However, I will not be conducting this interview. DC Stafford will be handling it. I think you know what it's about. See, despite so many people trying to blacken your name, I have nothing to hold you on myself. Ironic, really.'

'According to my client,' said the lawyer, 'this matter with the Americans is just a misunderstanding which can be very easily cleared as well.'

'I very much doubt that,' said Stafford.

'Anyway, Rob,' said Harris. 'I just have one outstanding matter to sort then I will leave you to it. It's just a pity that your father is not here.'

The words hung heavy in the air as Mackey stared at him.

'What did you say?' he said eventually.

'Your father. The venerated George. Now there was a man with something to hide.'

'You can't get me so you go after my father, is that it?' exclaimed Mackey. 'Bloody hell, man! You must be desperate. And if you say anything against my father ...'

'Does the name Edward Portland mean anything to you?'

asked Harris, removing a couple of pieces of paper from the brown file on the desk.

Mackey shook his head. 'No. Should it?'

'He was Lenny Portland's father.'

'He another drunk then?' said Mackey scornfully.

'I believe he was. Amazing how often the son turns out like the father, isn't it?'

Mackey glared at him.

'Now,' continued Harris, 'normally you would not expect the two men's paths to have crossed. Your father was, after all, a highly respected soldier with a chest full of medals and Edward Portland was, as you so delightfully pointed out, a drunk. However, in a small town like this I guess it was inevitable that they would meet from time to time. In fact, they had already had a couple of run-ins before the night in question, I believe.'

'Night? What night? What are you on about, man?' said Mackey but he sounded less confident.

Harris held up the pieces of paper.

'My sergeant found these earlier today,' he said. 'They do not mention your father's name but I believe they chronicle the last time he met Edward Portland. A matter of days before your father went out to the Falklands, in fact.'

It was not long after midnight when an inebriated Edward Portland lurched out of The Duck and into the deserted market place. As he staggered across the cobbles, he saw a set of headlights appear from his right but kept on walking until he was standing in the middle of the road. The vehicle slowed to a halt and the driver wound down his window.

'Get out of the way!' shouted George Mackey.

Portland swayed but did not move.

'Go on, get out of the way!' shouted the driver. 'Fucking drunk.'

Slowly, as deliberately as he could manage, Portland held

up two fingers. The driver rammed his foot on the accelerator and swerved past him, catching Portland a glancing blow with the wing mirror. Portland stumbled in the darkness and pitched forward. He did not feel what had hit him; at first he did not even know that he had been hit. Mind reeling, confused images swirling before his eyes, he sunk to his knees. He slowly turned his head, trying desperately to focus on the spinning world around him, trying to make sense of what had happened. Vision blurred, body now racked with jagged pain, he tried to stand up but his legs buckled and he staggered forward once more, this time to lie still and silent on the cold ground. Looking up, he saw a face staring down at him and heard a voice echoing as if from afar. The voice fell silent and the face receded into the distance as George Mackey strode back to his vehicle and the darkness closed in. The man was alone and he felt cold. He knew in that moment that he was dying. After that, he saw nothing, heard nothing, felt nothing. His was to sleep for ever. It was down to others to honour his memory.

In whatever way they saw fit.

'I vaguely remember something about it from the time,' said Harris as Mackey stared at him in silence, 'but it didn't really register. No one took much notice really. The coroner, a newly appointed Henry Maitlin, oddly enough, decided that Portland fell over and hit his head. A familiar story, eh? I take it you knew about this?'

'My father told me a couple of days before he went to join the Task Force,' said Mackey. His demeanour had changed. Now it was one of resignation and the edge that always existed between the men had gone. 'I have thought many times about that day. Never a day goes by ...'

He paused and the detectives let silence settle on the room, oppressive and enveloping.

'We were in the garden at Laurel House,' said Mackey

eventually, his voice slightly tremulous. 'Digging out an apple tree, as I recall. I was a teenager at the time. My father was not the type of man to confide in any member of his family, Inspector. He was not a particularly welcoming man, and the only reason I can think he did so then was that he knew he was not coming back from the Falklands. That somehow he knew and he wanted to unburden himself. Does that sound too fanciful a notion?'

'No, but why did he not come forward at the time? Surely he realized he had hit Ted Portland?'

'He did, yes. Even reversed up to see how he was.'

'Then all he had to do was come to us. There were no witnesses and if it was an accident, he had nothing to worry about.'

'You know what people are like round here. They hate anyone who's made something of themselves. Bloody ingrates. They'd have lynched him. You know that.' He gave a slight smile. 'Oddly enough, we have never been the most popular of families round here. Can you believe that?'

'Somehow, yes.'

'You know, I think he would have admitted everything if your lot had come for him – he always had a strong respect for authority – but they never did. After he was killed, it all seemed to go away.'

'You tell anyone else about this? Liz perhaps?'

'No one.' Mackey gave a mirthless laugh. 'Dark family secret, Inspector. Hardly the kind of thing you chat about at dinner parties. I say, I know Abigail has done awfully well at her ballet classes but my father killed a man.'

'Did you tell Alison Butterfield?'

'I wondered when you would mention her. No, I didn't. She knew nothing about it and I'm not just saying it to keep her out of trouble. Will I be able to see her after this?'

'From what I hear, she regards your affair as over.'

'I'm a bloody fool,' said Mackey with a shake of the head.

'A bloody fool. She was the best thing that ever happened to me.'

'Can we get back to your father?'

'I suppose we have to,' sighed Mackey. 'How did this come to light? Is it why the memorials are being vandalized?'

'We think so.'

'Lenny Portland doing it?'

'We're pretty sure he is, yes. We believe he only found out recently. We were rather hoping you might know who told him.'

'One of your lot, I assume. Roger Barnett.'

'Why him?'

'It would seem that he worked on the original inquiry and always had his suspicions about what happened. Apparently, someone thought they had seen my father's car out in the town not long after it happened but my father had gone to the Falklands by the time they came forward and after his death it all seemed to get forgotten.'

'There's nothing in the record about any of this. Roger Barnett is not even mentioned.'

'Not sure anyone was bothered really.' Mackey gave a slight smile. 'Like you said, drunk falls over and bangs head. A familiar story. The inquest took ten minutes, apparently. Besides, not long after my father left for the Falklands, Barnett went to work in Roxham and that was the last I heard of it.'

'Clearly Barnett did not forget it, though. He approach you?'

Mackey nodded.

'Why did he do that after all these years?' asked Harris.

'He called after it was announced that I was going to erect the memorial in Chapel Hill. Barnett said it was wrong, given what my father had done. I fobbed him off then the attacks started on the British Legion pavilion. I knew at once what it was about, of course. I guess Barnett told Lenny as a way of getting his own back.'

'But even then you did not come to us?'

'The last thing I wanted was you reopening the original inquiry so close to the unveiling.' Mackey gave another slight smile. 'Got to honour the dead whatever they've done, haven't we?'

'Talking of honouring the dead, your American pal took Harold Leach's VC home with him. Know anything about that?'

'No.'

'I think yes.'

'Prove it.'

'Maybe I will but in the meantime DC Stafford here wants to know more about our Mr Randall. Like I said, I'm mainly interested in Lenny Portland.'

Mackey gave a sigh. 'I had rather hoped that I would take this story to my grave,' he said. 'Like my father did.'

'You still might,' said Harris, slotting the piece of paper back in the file. 'Portland is missing, and we've just discovered that he's got a shotgun.'

'Surely you don't think he would do anything to harm me, though?'

'You been unpleasant to him lately?'

'Told him to get out of my way the odd time. The man's a drunk.'

'Funny how these things have a habit of coming back round on themselves, isn't it?' said Harris.

Mackey looked worried. 'Is there something you're not telling me?'

'Someone shot out the downstairs windows of your house less than an hour ago,' said Harris. 'Now who do you think would do a thing like that?'

There was a knock on the door and Gallagher walked in.

'He's here,' said the sergeant.

'Thank you,' said Harris, standing up and nodding at Stafford. 'I'll leave you to it.'

'Who's here?' asked Mackey anxiously.

Harris ignored the comment. He had just opened the door when a thought struck him and he looked back into the room.

'And yes,' he said, looking at Mackey, 'Liz and Bethany are all right.' Shaking his head, the inspector walked out of the room to join Matty Gallagher in walking along the corridor. 'I take it the search has not turned up any sign of Lenny Portland?'

'No, but it was only a perfunctory search. My thinking is to do a more detailed one of the town first then gradually fan out onto the hills.'

'Sounds sensible,' said Harris as they started down the stairs. 'You found our man then?'

'Yeah, but he's not desperately happy about it,' said Gallagher. 'Been banging on about Saturday being his day off.'

'Golf course?'

'Something like that,' said Gallagher as the officers walked into the interview room just off the reception area, where there sat a grey-haired, balding man in a red and white checked sweater.

'Are you Detective Chief Inspector Harris?' asked the man angrily.

'I am,' replied Harris, sitting down opposite him. 'You must be Dr Maddox.'

'Mr Maddox,' said the man tartly. 'Consultants are called Mr and might I say that this is all very irregular. How did you get hold of me?'

'Roxham Hospital let us have your number,' said Gallagher, also sitting down.

'Yes, well, they should not have done that. My normal working—'

'Lenny Portland,' interrupted Harris. 'One of his friends suggested that he may have been seeing a psychiatrist. That you?'

'As well you know, Inspector, we are unable to breach a patient's confidentiality. I am surprised that you of all people should—'

'Just answer the question, will you?'

'Why so interested?' said Maddox, glowering at the inspector.

'We believe he may have a gun and we want to find out if he is the type to use it.'

'Leonard?' said Maddox with a laugh. 'Use a gun? I think that is highly unlikely and even if—'

'We believe he shot out the windows of a house an hour ago.'

Maddox shook his head. 'Not Leonard,' he said.

'Well, someone did. Why did he come to see you, Mr Maddox?'

'I told you, patient conf—'

'I really do not have time for this,' snapped Harris. 'If you do not co-operate, so help me, I will arrest you for obstructing our inquiries.'

Maddox looked at him uncertainly then at Gallagher, as if seeking support from the sergeant.

'He will.' Gallagher nodded. 'And if he doesn't, I will. For wearing that sweater if nothing else. Just answer the questions, will you?'

Maddox considered the comment then nodded glumly.

'I have been seeing Leonard for fifteen years,' he said eventually, each word begrudged. 'Or rather, I saw him fifteen years ago for mild depression, probably linked to the amount of alcohol he had been consuming. He responded to treatment and was discharged after a matter of months.'

He hesitated.

'I sense a but,' said Harris.

'A few weeks ago, sometime in mid September, I think it was, the doctor's surgery up here referred him back to me. They believed Leonard may have been experiencing a reoccurrence of his previous problems. He had been acting somewhat erratically, apparently.'

'And *was* he experiencing some kind of relapse?'

'He was a touch fragile but it's difficult to be more precise on the exact nature of his condition.' The reply sounded vague, the consultant evasive.

'But you're the expert,' said Gallagher. 'Surely, if anyone would know, you would?'

Again, Maddox hesitated.

'Well?' said Gallagher.

'Look, Mr Maddox,' said Harris, leaning forward, 'I have got a man out there with a gun which he has already used once. I need to know everything I can about him.'

'He only came for his first appointment,' said Maddox in a voice so quiet the detectives could hardly hear it.

'What?' exclaimed Harris, glancing at Gallagher.

'He did not attend the follow-up ones,' said Maddox, adding quickly as he saw the sergeant shake his head in disbelief, 'We did not leave it there, of course. We wrote to him. Several times.'

'Perhaps we should write to him as well,' said Gallagher, the silence of the room disturbed by the clattering of rotor blades as the police helicopter swooped in low over Levton Bridge on its second sweep of the town. 'Let's just hope he gets it in time. Eh?'

The consultant gave him a sick look.

CHAPTER TWENTY-FOUR

The helicopter was still hovering over Levton Bridge when, having left Gallagher to co-ordinate the search for Lenny Portland, Jack Harris strode out of the police station and up the hill towards the courtroom. Long before he reached the market place, the inspector could hear the raised voices of the angry crowd that had gathered. Turning the corner, the DCI was confronted by more than fifty people standing outside the court building. He recognized many of them; some he had never seen before. Among them was Henry Maitlin. As the detective worked his way through the crowd, he was approached by Elaine Landy and a cameraman.

'Inspector,' she said as the cameraman focused on him, 'do you have any comment on the arrest of the men for...?'

'You know better than that,' said Harris. 'Never heard of sub judice?'

'Yes, but surely you can...?'

Harris brushed past her, blocking the camera lens with his hand, and walked through the front door of the courtroom. Two minutes later, he was sitting on the same bench he had occupied for the inquest into Philip Morritt's death earlier in the week. A lot had happened since then, he thought. Still could, he thought, catching a glimpse of the helicopter through one of the windows. Harris turned his attention to the public gallery, which was already full of people waiting to see Forrest and Michaels. They did not have long to wait as the magistrates duly filed in to take their seats. All eyes turned to the dock and an angry murmuring ran round the room when the accused men were brought up, Forrest looking calm despite his situation and Michaels had a livid blue bruise on his cheek. Both men caught sight of the inspector. Forrest scowled. Michaels looked away.

'Bastards!' yelled someone and there were shouts of agreement.

'Ladies and gentlemen,' said the chairwoman of the bench, 'please restrain yourselves or I will have the courtroom cleared.'

The room fell silent.

'Thank you,' she said. 'This is a special sitting following the arrest of David Forrest and Ronald Michaels in connection with the murder of Harold Leach. Mr Haines appears for ...'

Five minutes later, it was all over and Harris strode back into the market-place, pointedly ignoring the waiting cameraman. Seeing Butterfield standing next to a couple of uniformed constables in front of one of the shops, he walked over to join her and, without talking, they surveyed the crowd for a few moments. There was an angry sound as word spread that the prison van had edged itself out of the alley behind the courtroom and was on its way up the hill towards the market place. People surged forward as the van appeared and the driver was forced to slow down as several men banged on the side of the vehicle. Harris caught sight of Henry Maitlin; his face was twisted with hate.

A couple of press photographers held up their cameras to try to get a shot of the suspects through the blacked-out windows then turned their attention to the shaven-headed young man who was trying to wrench open the van's door, only to be pulled back by a couple of uniformed officers.

'That's Billy Duggan, isn't it?' said Butterfield as he was

hauled away, lashing out at the officer holding him. 'He's not normally violent.'

'Like I kept trying to tell folks, anything is possible.' Harris glanced up at the hovering helicopter and started walking towards the police station. 'Anything.'

Ten minutes later, he walked into the briefing room, which was packed with a large number of officers, some local, many drafted in from surrounding areas. All eyed him expectantly as he walked to the front of the room. Harris surveyed the faces; Gallagher over by the window, staring down at the row of police vans parked in the street, Gillian Roberts in the front row next to Butterfield and Larch, Curtis sitting at the back, slightly apart from everyone else. And Roger Barnett, leaning against the wall with a grim expression on his face. Harris turned to the board and tapped the large photograph that had been pinned up.

'Lenny Portland,' he said. 'This is our boy, ladies and gentlemen. Until he shot out the windows of Laurel House, he was viewed as little more than a harmless petty thief with a drink problem. Now it seems that he may be a little more than that.'

'How dangerous is he?' asked one of the officers. 'He likely to have a pop at us?'

'We have to assume that to be the case. Trouble is, the shrink has not seen him for two months. The concern has to be that, in his current state, anything could set him off. Unfortunately' – and Harris looked across at Barnett – 'we believe that someone did just that. Eh, Roger?'

Everyone stared at the sergeant, who looked down at his shoes.

'Our biggest concern,' said Harris, 'is that Lenny may be thinking about disrupting tomorrow's Remembrance Day ceremony. Our job is to get to him before then. OK, on your way. Let's get him found. Oh, and be careful. This lad's a crackerjack.'

With a loud murmuring and the scraping of chair legs, the search teams headed for the door. As Barnett made to follow them, Curtis approached him.

'Roger,' said the commander, 'might I have a word?'

As the police teams searched gardens and outhouses, streets and parks, pub cellars and the back rooms of shops, Jack Harris, accompanied by Butterfield, headed for Lenny Portland's terraced house on the edge of town. Nodding to the uniformed officer at the front door, Harris walked into the hallway, wrinkling his nose at the smell. The carpet was threadbare and stained in places and a pile of old newspapers stood at the bottom of the stairs, next to several empty beer bottles. Harris walked into the equally untidy living room as Butterfield went to search the upstairs bedrooms. Alone in the room, the inspector let silence settle.

'Come on, Lenny,' he murmured, 'where are you, son?'

After three minutes, Butterfield came downstairs and walked into the room.

'Anything?' asked Harris.

'Nothing. Smells terrible as well. Should see the toilet.'

'I can imagine.'

'How did we miss this, guv?' she asked, glancing at him. 'How did I miss it? I mean, I probably had more to do with Lenny than anyone and yet I did not see it coming. Just did not see it coming.'

'I wouldn't beat yourself up about it, Constable, none of us did. Even Barry Gough knew nothing about any of this. Said if he had known how unstable he was, he would never have given him the shotgun.'

The inspector's mobile rang and he listened for a few moments, mumbled a 'thanks' and returned the phone to his pocket.

'That was James Larch,' he said. 'Bob who runs the fishing tackle shop off Rainer Street reckons he sold some shotgun cartridges to Lenny yesterday.'

'I feel like I've cocked up big-time.' She seemed close to tears.

'When I was in the army,' said Harris, walking over to the front window and watching as two uniformed officers started door-to-door at the end of the street, 'I was stationed in Germany at one point. There was this fellow. Little chap he was. No one ever took any notice of him. Hardly ever spoke, never got into arguments. Then one day the sergeant said something to him, I forget what it was, and this little chap went for him. Put him in hospital with a fractured skull, trashed the mess and assaulted three MPs.' Harris gave her a reassuring smile. 'So you see, despite what an ageing chief inspector might say, sometimes you just cannot read the situation, however hard you try.'

'Thank you,' she said and gave him a little smile.

His phone rang. 'It's DC Stafford,' said a voice. 'We are going to bail Rob Mackey. He wants to see you before he goes.'

Twenty minutes later, the inspector was back in the interview room, sitting next to Stafford and staring across the table at Mackey and his solicitor.

'You wanted to see me,' said Harris.

'I wanted you to know that I intend to be at the Remembrance Sunday ceremony tomorrow.'

'Are you sure that's wise? We still have not found Lenny Portland.'

'I go every year, to honour my father.'

'Even though you know what he did?'

'Even though I know what he did. Besides, Henry Maitlin asked me some time ago if I would lay a wreath in memory of the men of Chapel Hill. Are you going to stop me?'

'It's a free country, Rob,' said Harris. 'Isn't that what they all died for? You do what you want.'

Mackey gave a thin smile. 'Does that make me bait?' he asked.

Jack Harris did not reply.

Shortly before seven, he was sitting in his office, feet up on the desk, eyes closed. His dogs lay curled up in their usual position beneath the radiator.

'A fine way to spend Saturday night, eh, boys?' said the inspector, glancing down at the dogs. 'When this is done and dusted, we'll finish that walk over Howgill Top. Promise.'

Archie struggled to his feet and wagged his tail. Scoot did not acknowledge the comment. The inspector's desk phone rang.

'It's Henry,' said a voice when he picked up the receiver. 'Have you got him?'

'Sorry, Henry. They're still out there but we're pretty sure he's not in the town and there's not much we can do in the countryside with it being dark. There's always the chance that he took fright after what happened at Laurel House and is no longer in the area.'

'Can you promise me that?'

'You know the answer, Henry.'

'Then I have no alternative but to call off tomorrow,' said Maitlin quietly. 'Your Superintendent Curtis said we had to make a decision by seven and it's nearly that now. I mean, what if he tries to kill Rob Mackey?'

'Who, the superintendent?'

'This is no time for jokes, Jack.'

'Sorry, Henry. I've told Mackey he can attend if he wants. He's keen to be there. You asked him to lay a wreath, I think.'

'To the men of Chapel Hill, yes, but ...' Maitlin's voice tailed off. He sounded lost. 'What would you do, Jack?'

'I'd go ahead. Any other event I'd have said no but this is Remembrance Sunday, Henry. Those guys would not have accepted defeat and neither should we.'

'If you're sure.' Maitlin did not sound convinced.

'I'm sure, Henry.'

'I'll tell him I want to go ahead then,' said Maitlin. 'Just make sure nothing happens.'

'No pressure there then,' murmured Harris as he ended the call just as Philip Curtis walked into the room.

Harris thought the commander had a look on his face that was different from their usual confrontations. Friendly, thought the DCI. No, not friendly, never friendly. Harris would not want it to be friendly. So what then? Understanding, possibly. Yes, understanding.

'You and your team have done really well,' said Curtis, sitting down at the desk.

'Enough results for you, sir?' asked Harris with a slight smile.

'Almost. I've just had the military police on singing your praises. Not to mention Harold Leach's granddaughter almost in tears because you caught Forrest and Michaels. Oh, and a DI called Standish—'

'What did he say?' asked Harris quickly.

'Grateful that you helped him clear up a crime in his area. You've been busy.' Curtis nodded at the phone. 'Who was that? Another happy customer?'

'Not quite. Henry Maitlin. I suspect he is about to ring you.'

'What did you tell him?'

'That if it was down to me, I would go ahead with tomorrow's ceremony.'

'I agree with you. The chief's not so sure but I am.'

'You are?'

'I do agree with you sometimes, Jack. But only when there's an R in the month.'

Harris chuckled. He could not remember ever having done that with Philip Curtis.

'It's a gamble, though,' said the commander, serious again. 'We don't know where Lenny Portland is and there's no guarantee we'll find him before tomorrow.'

'Granted but we should be able to secure the place OK. The weapons boys seem fairly confident. I just think it would be wrong to cancel it. Send out the wrong message.'

Curtis nodded and there was silence. It was broken by Harris.

'What have you done with Barnett?' he asked.

'Suspended him pending a full investigation. Told him he should have come to me if he wanted to bring the Portland thing up again. He tried to argue that he was only trying to do the right thing but it didn't wash, Jack, it really didn't. It may be quite some time before he hooks up with Sergeant Squirrel.'

'Sir?'

'It's going to be his next challenge if he gets through this. Road safety.'

'Appropriate.'

'That's what I thought.' Curtis stood up. 'Listen, Jack, I know you and me have not always got on.'

'You could say that.'

'But I appreciate what you do, even if I do not always agree with how you do it.' Curtis looked at the dogs. 'And even if I hate them with a rare passion.'

Scoot gave him a dirty look and Archie whimpered. Curtis ignored them and headed out into the corridor. He popped his head back into the office.

'But if you tell anyone I said something nice to you,' he said, 'I will have to kill you. Have I made that clear?'

'Crystal,' said Harris, grinning. When the sound of the

commander's footsteps had faded away, the inspector glanced down at the dogs. 'You think you know someone, eh?'

As the first rays of light streaked the dawn sky, Jack Harris and Matty Gallagher waited in a car park on the edge of Levton Bridge and watched as the force helicopter touched down on the tarmac, the clatter of its rotor blades disturbing the Sunday-morning peace. Within seconds, the detectives were aboard and the aircraft was rising into the sky before turning to sweep low across the town, the wan early-morning light revealing teams of uniforms fanning out from the police station. As the helicopter wheeled over the town, Harris looked down on deserted streets and gardens.

'Anything?' he shouted to Gallagher, who was on the other side of the craft.

Gallagher shook his head.

'Where the hell is he?' murmured Harris.

The helicopter banked and headed north out of town to fly low over fields and hillsides, the officers looking down on sheep huddled in the lee of dry-stone walls, copses waving in the breeze and chuckling brooks dancing their way down grassy slopes. Harris tapped Gallagher on the shoulder and pointed to a line of red shapes working their way along one of the ravines.

'The mountain rescue boys,' shouted the inspector. 'They were out just after six looking for him.'

'If Portland's here, we should have found him by now. Maybe he's not. Maybe we've got away with—'

The pilot turned round.

'Message for you, Inspector,' he said. 'One of the ground teams has found something.'

'On the other hand,' said Gallagher.

The helicopter touched down in a farmyard on the edge of Levton Bridge and the two detectives jumped out and ran across to a barn outside of which stood two uniformed officers.

'Where is it?' asked Harris.

'Inside,' said one of the uniforms, directing them to an old tarpaulin next to which lay a couple of sweet wrappers and an empty beer bottle.

'When did you find them?' asked Harris, glancing at the farmer who had just walked into the barn.

''Bout twenty minutes ago.' He looked worried. 'Do you reckon he's been here, Mr Harris?'

Harris looked round the barn. 'He's been here,' he said grimly.

'You want to call the ceremony off?' asked Gallagher. 'There's still time.'

Harris shook his head. 'No,' he said. 'This town has pledged to honour its dead and honour them it will.'

'Just as long as it doesn't add anyone else to the list.'

'He'll not get into the market place,' said Harris and walked out of the barn.

As the town clock edged its way closer to the eleven, uniformed teams began to take up positions around the square, watching as people started to filter in from the side streets. The atmosphere was in stark contrast to the previous afternoon. Gone was the anger; many people looked uneasily about them, unnerved by the heavy police presence and the clattering of the helicopter yet determined to support the war veterans.

Several armed officers took up discreet positions in shop doorways and one officer carrying a rifle emerged onto a rooftop and stared down at the rapidly filling market place.

And all the time, the force helicopter hovered above the market place, the chatter of its rotors filling the air. At ten to eleven, Jack Harris walked into the square and took up his position, leaning in the doorway of one of the tearooms, soon to be joined by Matty Gallagher.

'Nothing?' asked the inspector.

'I don't reckon he's going to show.' Gallagher surveyed the crowd. 'Remarkable turnout.'

Harris nodded. 'Right decision,' he said.

As the clock ticked over onto five-to, the detectives could hear the sound of music and a long line of war veterans marched proudly into the square, led by a local brass band. Arms swinging, medals glinting in the morning sun, Henry Maitlin at their head, just a few paces ahead of Rob Mackey, the veterans made their way to the war memorial, Philip Curtis a few steps back in dress uniform, walking next to the mayor. The band stopped playing and the helicopter wheeled away, the sound of the rotor blades fading into the distance. Silence settled on the market place.

'If he is here, he'll make his move now,' whispered Harris, as Rob Mackey, clutching his wreath, took his place among the war veterans gathered round the memorial.

'I've never known anything like it,' said Gallagher. His mouth felt dry. 'Have you?'

'Once or twice.' Harris glanced up at the rooftops.

'You reckon he might be up there?'

'Old habits die hard, Matty lad. Saw a man taken out by a sniper in Cyprus once. Clean between the eyes.'

'Yeah, thanks for making me feel better.'

Harris waved to the armed officer on the roof and returned his attention to Henry Maitlin, who along with the mayor stepped forward and placed his wreath at the base of the memorial. Representatives of the three armed forces did likewise, followed by Rob Mackey, who glanced nervously to right and left as he did so.

'Say what you like about him,' murmured Gallagher, 'but that takes bottle.'

Harris did not reply as the haunting sound of 'The Last Post' drifted across the market place.

'Never hear that without feeling the hairs on the back of my neck rise,' he said as the final notes faded away.

'A no-show then,' said Gallagher, relief in his voice as the brass band struck up again, the veterans turned and marched from the market place and the crowd started to drift away.

'So it would seem,' said Harris. But he did not sound convinced.

The detectives followed the procession down the hill towards the police station, where the band stopped playing and the veterans started to disperse. As the detectives reached the steps of the station, Curtis caught up with them.

'Well done, Jack,' he said. 'A fine operation.'

'Thank you, sir.'

Rob Mackey walked over to them and extended his hand to the inspector.

'Thank you,' he said. 'Thank you for keeping me safe.'

Harris hesitated then, on noticing everyone watching him, grudgingly shook the hand. Mackey walked down the hill towards his Range Rover, which was parked on the pavement.

'Perhaps we can give him a ticket for blocking the public highway,' said Harris. Noticing the commander's look, he feigned innocence. 'What? What have I said?'

'Now, now, Jack,' said Curtis as he walked up the steps, adding over his shoulder, 'Just you behave.'

But they could tell he was smiling.

'You and he big buddies now then?' asked Gallagher.

Before Harris could reply, the detectives were joined by Alison Butterfield and the three detectives stood at the bottom of the steps and watched Mackey as he took his car keys from a coat pocket and unlocked the vehicle.

'It definitely over then?' Harris asked her as Mackey took off his coat and placed it carefully on the back seat. 'You and lover boy history?'

She nodded. 'I went to see his wife last night.'

'Yeah?'

'Yes, when we had finished the search. Told her what I had done.'

'What'd she say?' asked Gallagher.

'Think she was glad to see the back of him, but the daughter, she gave me a filthy look. Not sure I blame her.'

Mackey made as if to get into the driver's seat then saw Butterfield. For a moment, their eyes met then the constable turned away and Mackey got into his car and started the engine. After doing a three-point turn, he headed towards the crossroads and the officers turned to walk up the steps. They had just reached the front door when they heard shouting, a woman's scream and the squealing of tyres. Staring down the hill, they saw Lenny Portland standing in the middle of the road, his shotgun trained on the Range Rover, which had come to a halt a few metres away. The detectives sprinted down the hill, barging their way past startled war veterans and families.

'Don't no one come any closer!' shouted Portland in a trembling voice as he saw them walking slowly down the left-hand side of the car. 'Just don't no one come any closer.'

'Come on, Lenny,' said Harris, glancing into the vehicle where an ashen-faced Mackey was staring in horror, his knuckles glowing white as he gripped the steering wheel.

Harris took another step forward.

'You stay back!' Portland turned the gun to point at the inspector.

Harris stopped walking. 'Have it your way, Lenny,' he said.

'I don't want to hurt you,' said Portland, turning the gun back towards Mackey. 'I don't want to hurt no one but him.'

Mackey looked even more frightened.

'But why, Lenny?' asked Harris.

217

'Because of what happened to my father.' He seemed close to tears.

'Think it through, son. Rob didn't do that, did he? It was his father. Thirty years ago.'

'Yeah, but he knew.' Portland started crying and lowered the gun slightly. He lifted it again as he saw armed officers edging their way down the streets, which was now virtually deserted as others ushered the crowds away. 'Keep them back or I'll shoot!'

Harris turned and gestured to the armed officers, who stopped walking.

'We'll play it your way, Lenny,' he said, 'but it makes no sense to kill Rob for what his father did.'

'No?' said Portland bitterly, tears starting to flow now. 'He knew but he never told anyone. Do you know how old I were when it happened? Do you?'

'No.'

'Twelve, that's how old. That's no age to lose your father. Someone has to pay for what happened.'

'If you pull that trigger,' said Harris, glancing behind him at the armed officers 'they will drop you where you stand.'

Portland hesitated then lifted the gun again, gripping it even tighter.

'No,' he said, voice firmer. 'No ...'

'Lenny,' said Alison Butterfield softly, brushing past the inspector. 'Give it up, love.'

Portland seemed to waver slightly.

'Why should I?' he said but he sounded less sure of himself.

'Because you need help. And because we let you down.' Butterfield glanced at Mackey, who still gripped the steering wheel, unable to take his eyes off the shotgun. 'We all let you down, love.'

Portland looked hopefully at her. 'Will you get me help?' he said, tears streaming down his cheeks.

'I promise,' said Butterfield.

Portland hesitated then nodded and lowered the gun. Butterfield walked forward and took it off him.

'We'll get it right this time,' she said, placing an arm round his shoulder. 'I promise.'

Two uniformed officers rushed forward and grabbed Portland, twisting his arms behind his back so that he squealed with pain.

'Be careful with him,' protested Butterfield.

'Yeah, lads,' shouted Harris as they led Portland up the hill. 'Go easy!'

Butterfield shot him a grateful look and walked back towards her colleagues.

'Well done, Constable,' said Harris, patting her on the shoulder.

'Thank you, sir.' She was trembling. 'At least I got one thing right. I kind of feel like I made up for ... well, you know.'

'I do indeed. For a start, it means I do not have to live with the knowledge that I saved your ex-boyfriend's life.' He headed up the hill. 'Can you believe how hard that would be? Doesn't bear thinking about, just doesn't bear thinking about.'

Butterfield watched him go then looked across at Gallagher.

'Can you believe him sometimes?' she said with a shake of the head.

Gallagher nodded. 'Yeah,' he said. 'Yeah, I reckon I can.'

'This is where it belongs,' said Maggie, looking at the VC in a glass case, sitting on a crimson cushion next to a black and white photograph of Harold Leach in uniform and a faded newspaper cutting telling the story of his wartime bravery. 'This is where my grandfather's medal should be. It needs to be seen.'

'Indeed,' said Harris, nodding.

It was mid-morning and they were standing in one of the rooms at Roxham Museum. Around them milled a mixture of civic dignitaries and war veterans, all there for the opening of the new exhibition devoted to the area's war heroes. Glancing at the next case, Harris noticed that it was devoted to George Mackey's Military Cross, which sat on a cushion as well. The inspector looked round the room and frowned. Only the previous day, Rob had been extradited to stand trial in America and there had been no sign of Liz or Bethany at the courthouse in Manchester. They were not at the opening of the exhibition either.

'So much for honouring the dead,' murmured Harris.

'Sorry?'

'Nothing. Just thinking aloud.'

'My grandfather would have been very embarrassed at all this, you know,' said Maggie, accepting a glass of orange juice from a young woman who was circulating with a tray. She looked across at the local councillors talking to the chief constable. 'He hated fuss.'

'Not quite his thing, I imagine,' said Harris, following her gaze.

'Not really. Stuffed shirts, he used to call them.'

'I knew there was a reason I liked him.' The inspector's mobile rang. Gallagher, said the read-out. Harris lifted the device to his ear. 'Matty lad, can't you manage without me for a couple of hours?'

'Sorry,' said the sergeant; Harris could hear that his colleague was trying not to laugh. 'Roger Barnett and Sergeant Squirrel are making an appearance at the primary school this afternoon and Curtis wondered if you fancied popping along? Thinks we should be officially represented. Would have gone himself but he reckons you might derive more satisfaction from the experience.'

Gallagher lost his battle with laughter. So did Jack Harris.